Raven Girl

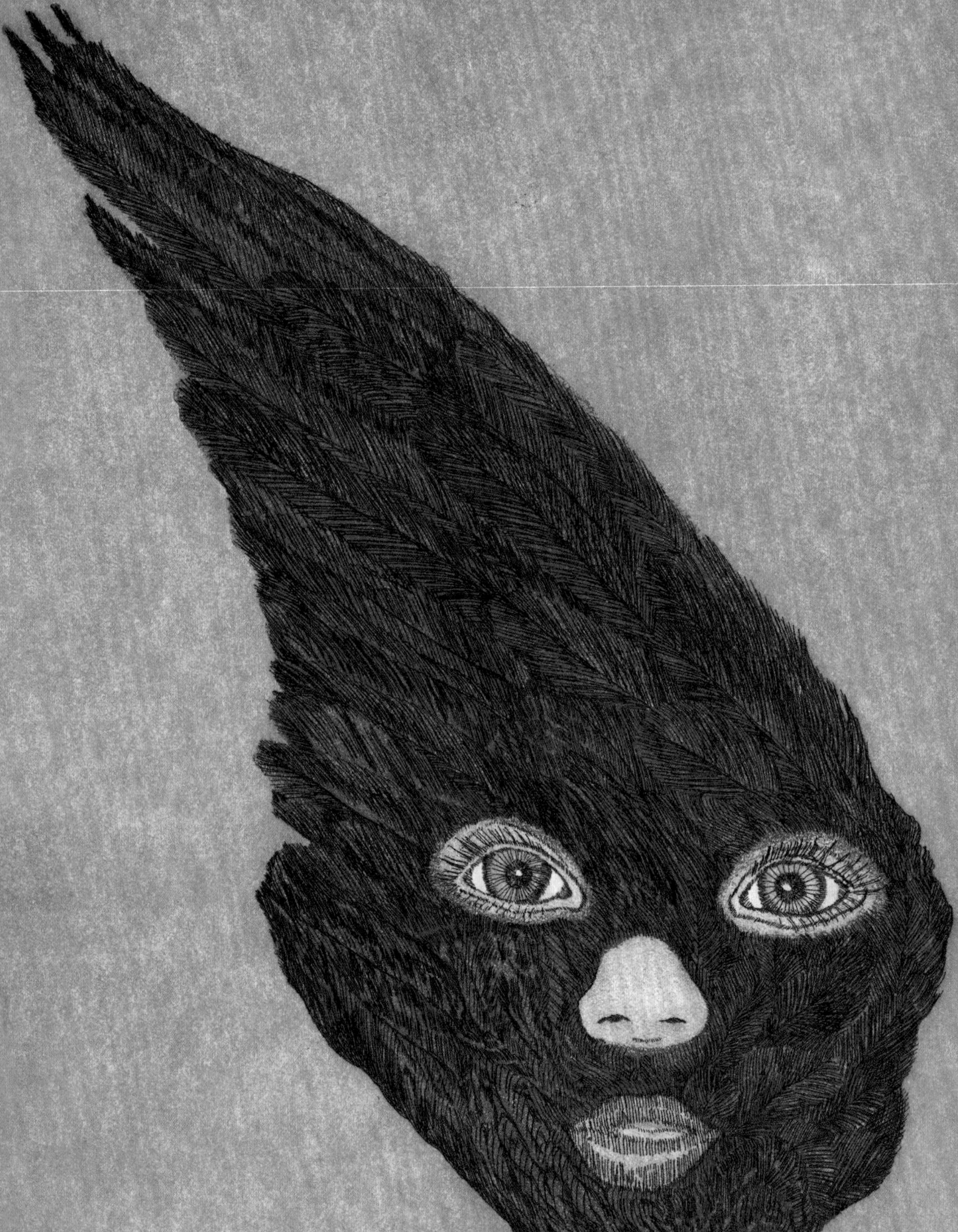

Raven Girl

AUDREY NIFFENEGGER

Jonathan Cape • London

Published by Jonathan Cape 2013

10 9 8 7 6 5 4 3 2 1

First published in North America by Abrams ComicArts, an imprint
of ABRAMS. All rights reserved.

First published in Great Britain in 2013 by
Jonathan Cape
Random House, 20 Vauxhall Bridge Road, London SW1V 2SA

www.vintage-books.co.uk

Addresses for companies within The Random House Group Limited
can be found at: www.randomhouse.co.uk/offices.htm

The Random House Group Limited Reg. No. 954009

A CIP catalogue record for this book is available from the British Library

ISBN 9780224097871

Printed and bound in China

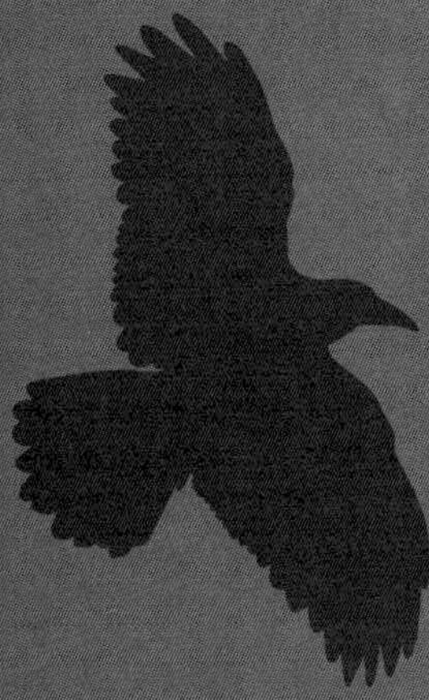

nce there was a Postman who fell in love with a Raven.

The Postman lived on the edge of a flat, desolate suburb. When he looked to the west he could see the skyscrapers of the city of which his suburb was the outermost appendage. When he looked east he saw flat, bare land that stretched away from his home until it met the cliffs that stood over even starker, more desolate places.

His house was very small. There were no trees around it and no birds. Once in a while a rabbit came by and ate all the strawberries in his little garden.

The Postman had been a postman for quite a few years. He was no longer a young and ardent postman; he thought he had seen just about everything Her Majesty's Postal Service could offer in the way of danger and difficulty, hilarity and boredom. He yearned to have an adventure, but he suspected that he probably wouldn't. Every day he sorted his mail and put it in his sack and walked his round. Then he went home, had his tea, watched TV, and fell asleep on the sofa. He sometimes had nightmares that featured e-mail.

On a particularly rainy Monday morning in April, the Postman was sorting mail when he found a letter with an address he had never seen before. The letter was stamped *Special Delivery*. It was addressed in an elegant hand that suggested it might have been mailed in a previous century.

Dripping Rock, Ravens' Nest
2 Flat Drab Manor
East Underwhelm, Otherworld
EE1 LH9

EE1 LH9? The postcode made no sense. The letter had gone astray. He brought it to his supervisor, a venerable lady who had been with the Postal Service since before the invention of the penny post. She examined the address closely, raising and lowering her spectacles several times to inspect it. She handed it back to the Postman.

"East of East, Lower Heights," she told him. "It is, I'm afraid, on your walk."

"How odd," replied the Postman. "I never had a letter to deliver there before." He felt as one does when dreaming about familiar houses with sudden strange rooms discovered in unlikely places. It was as though he had found a train station attached to his kitchen.

"They don't receive much mail," his supervisor admitted. The return address merely said *Pinfeathers, West Farther*, which didn't illuminate the situation.

"Well," said the Postman. He finished sorting his mail and put it in his sack. He walked his round. The weather got a bit brighter. The Postman thought, *It's not a bad day for a long walk.* He felt a slight thrill at the prospect of a new address.

He set out for East of East, Lower Heights. It lay in the direction of his home, and he passed the tiny house with a pang. As he walked, he whistled. Once in a while something whistled back. There must be birds, but where? Things were moving at the edge of his vision. Spring was trying to come even to these flat places, and the Postman began to see heather and trees in the distance. The bird sounds became louder, surrounding him, but still he saw no birds.

After two hours of uneventful walking he came to the cliffs. He looked for a house but saw none; there were only the cliffs and the flatlands. He looked up, thinking that perhaps the house was on top of the cliffs. But all he saw was an enormous nest, tucked onto a ledge on the side of a cliff. He looked at the address on the envelope: *Dripping Rock, Ravens' Nest*. The rocks were somewhat drippy, and the nest was certainly big enough to accommodate ravens.

"Hello?" said the Postman. He could hear squabbling coming from the nest. He stood beneath it, unsure if it would be a good idea to attract attention to himself.

Just then he heard a little squawk. He looked down and saw a fledgling raven huddled at his feet. She raised her head and opened her beak, as though soundlessly imploring him. The din from the nest was louder now. He propped the letter at the base of the cliff and bent over the Raven. She shook her wings and looked at him with curiosity.

"Are you broken?" he asked her. She didn't understand; she had fallen out of the nest, but she wasn't broken. She was just resting and wondering how she might get back up and into the nest. She had also been wondering when her parents would return and what they would bring her for dinner.

Her brothers yelled at her from the nest. They made unflattering comments about the Postman, whom they mistook for a cat; none of them had seen a person before, and cats featured in all the scary stories their parents told them at bedtime.

Cats are not to be trusted! Cats will pounce on you and eat you!

Watch out! her brothers yelled. They beat their wings and made terrible noises, but none of them flew down to help her: They couldn't fly yet.

The Raven was frightened.

The cat, or whatever it was, loomed over her and looked interested. The Raven closed her eyes and prepared to be eaten.

The Postman misinterpreted this. "Oh, dear," he said. He thought the Raven looked ill. He picked her up. Her heart was beating very fast. He wrapped her in his scarf and began the long walk home, the Raven trembling in his arms.

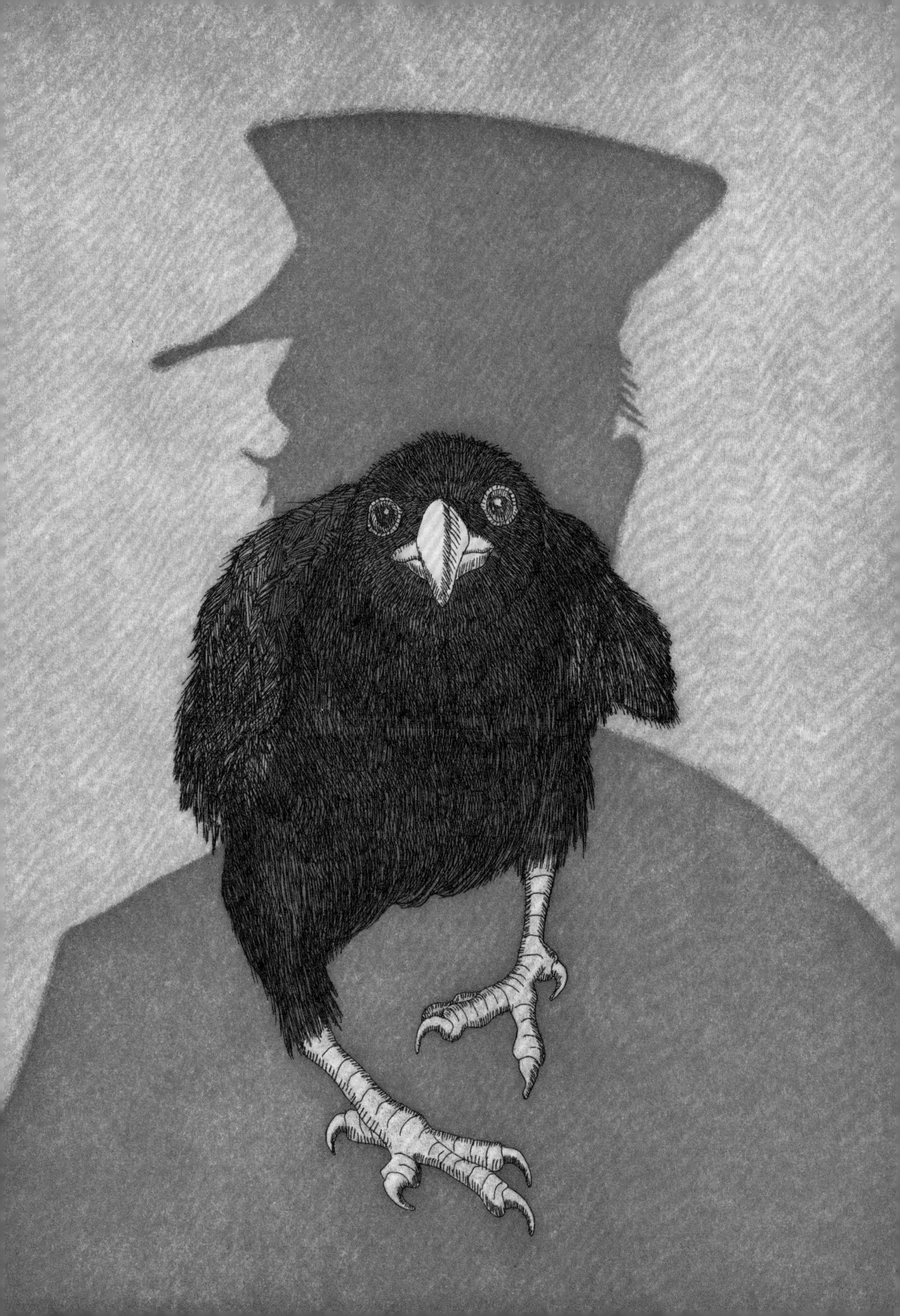

hen the Raven's parents returned to the nest they asked, "Where is your sister?" Her brothers said, "She fell out of the nest, and a cat found her and took her away." The parents were grieved and puzzled by this, and they searched for the Raven for a long time. Whenever they saw a cat, they asked it where their daughter was, but all the cats swore they didn't know, which only confirmed the perfidiousness of cats.

———— ▶▶◀◀ ————

he Postman tended to the Raven carefully. He made her a nest out of his old uniforms and shredded junk mail, and she lived on his kitchen table. He fed her sardines, earthworms, eggs,

cheese, Weetabix, and raw lamb chops. He brought
her snails and road-killed squirrels. He talked to
her. He discovered that he liked having someone to
talk to. She talked back, but he didn't understand
her raven language of harsh caws and soft croaks.
Sometimes she mimicked him, but he wasn't sure
if that meant anything.

At first the Raven longed for her mother and
father and brothers, and she kept an eye on the sky
outside the kitchen window. But no ravens came to
find her. As the days and weeks went by the Raven
was charmed by the Postman. She understood
that he meant no harm and that he was not a cat.
She learned some of his language. She developed
a fondness for television and junk food.

Slowly the Raven and the Postman began to
fall in love.

The Raven loved the Postman's big goofy smile and his ginger hair. She liked to ride on his shoulder and talk into his ear. He was a gentle man, and she fell in love with his quiet ways and his hands, deft and wondrous to her, hands that could open jars and doors, hands that stroked her head and smoothed her feathers.

The Postman was amazed by the intelligence and grace of the Raven. As she grew and lived in his house and watched him, she began to perform little tasks for him; she might stir the soup, or finish a jigsaw puzzle; she could find his keys (or hide them, for the fun of watching him hunt for them). She was like a wife to him, solicitous of his moods, patient with his stories of postal triumph and tragedy. She grew large and sleek, and he wondered how he would live without her when the time came for her to fly away.

Summer arrived, and the Raven stretched her wings and beat them in the air, rising a few feet from the kitchen floor. The Postman opened the back door, and she walked outside. "Go ahead," he said, longing to see her fly, afraid she couldn't, desperate to keep her and ashamed of this. She beat her wings and looked back at him. He gestured to her: *Up, up.* His smile was pathetic. She tried again and flew across the garden. He applauded, startling her. "It's okay," he said. "Don't mind me." She looked at the sky and back at the Postman. Then she flew.

Up, up! There was no one to tell her how to do it—somehow her raven body knew. She was clumsy, unpractised, but she flew; the air held her, and she rose into it. The Postman watched and felt joy—and despair. Now he would be alone again. The Raven vanished, and he still stood watching the sky.

Then he saw her. She circled and saw him and cried out. He held out his arms; she nearly knocked him over trying to land on his hand. "You came back," he said to her, marvelling. She didn't understand the words; why was he surprised? This was her home, where else would she go? The Postman opened the back door, and she walked inside. He gave her filet mignon and blueberries for supper. She sat on his shoulder and rubbed her head against his ear. She sang little soft songs that the Postman didn't understand. Then he got it. Blushing deeply he said, "Yes, yes—," and though he felt extremely strange proposing marriage to a raven, he did it anyway.

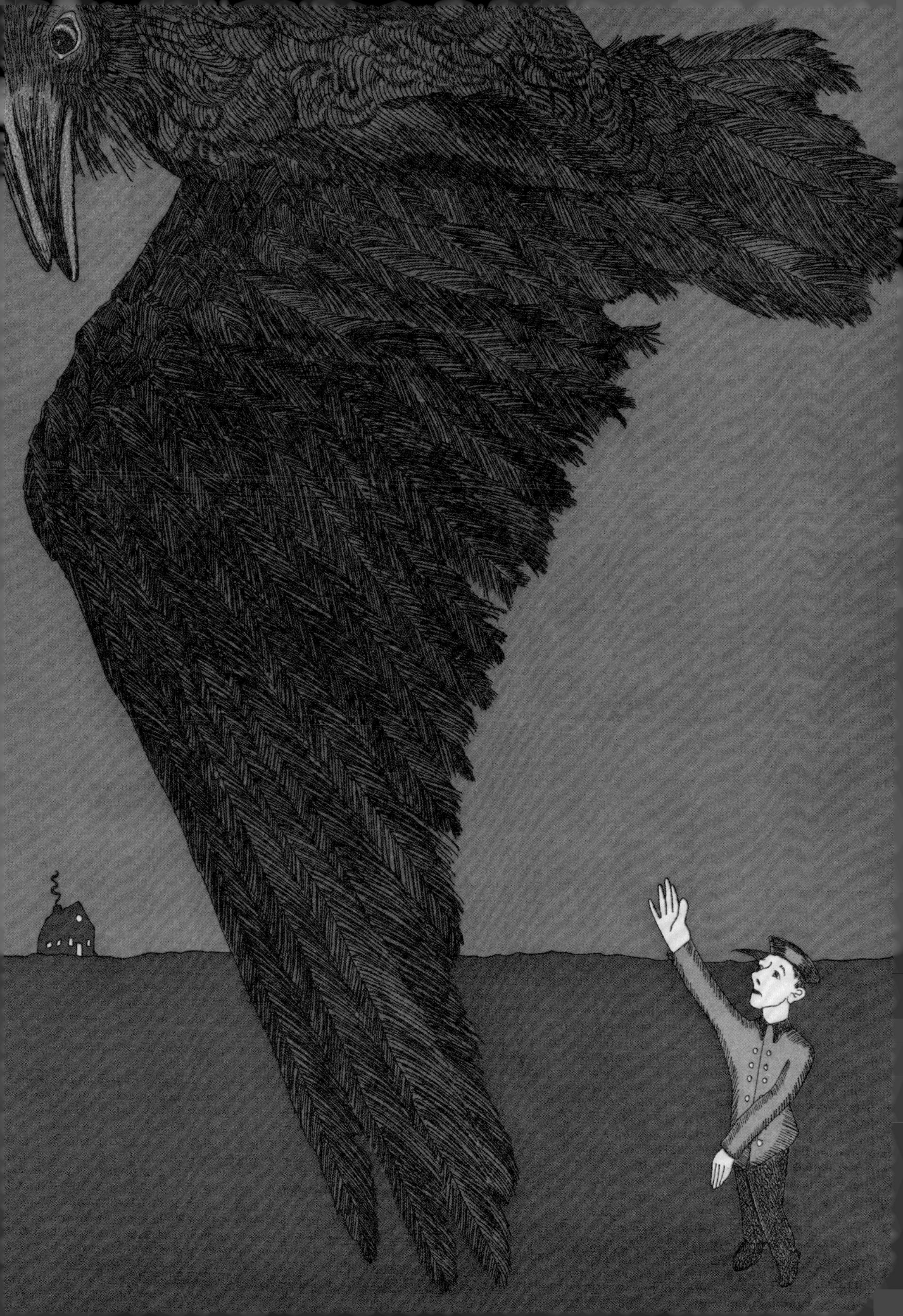

"Yes, yes," she replied, and though he thought she couldn't understand, he was happy and so was she.

———◦▸▸•◂◂◦———

The egg was greenish-bluish with brown speckles. The Raven had built a sumptuous nest for the egg out of tinfoil, magazines, sticks, and moss. At first the egg seemed small and lost in the nest. The Raven brooded over the egg, and the Postman hovered around anxiously. "Can I get you anything? Cheese? More tinfoil?" He wondered what a male raven ought to be doing. But the Raven seemed content.

The egg was peculiar. Whenever the Postman happened to get a glimpse of it, it seemed to him slightly larger. Sometimes he thought it was watching him.

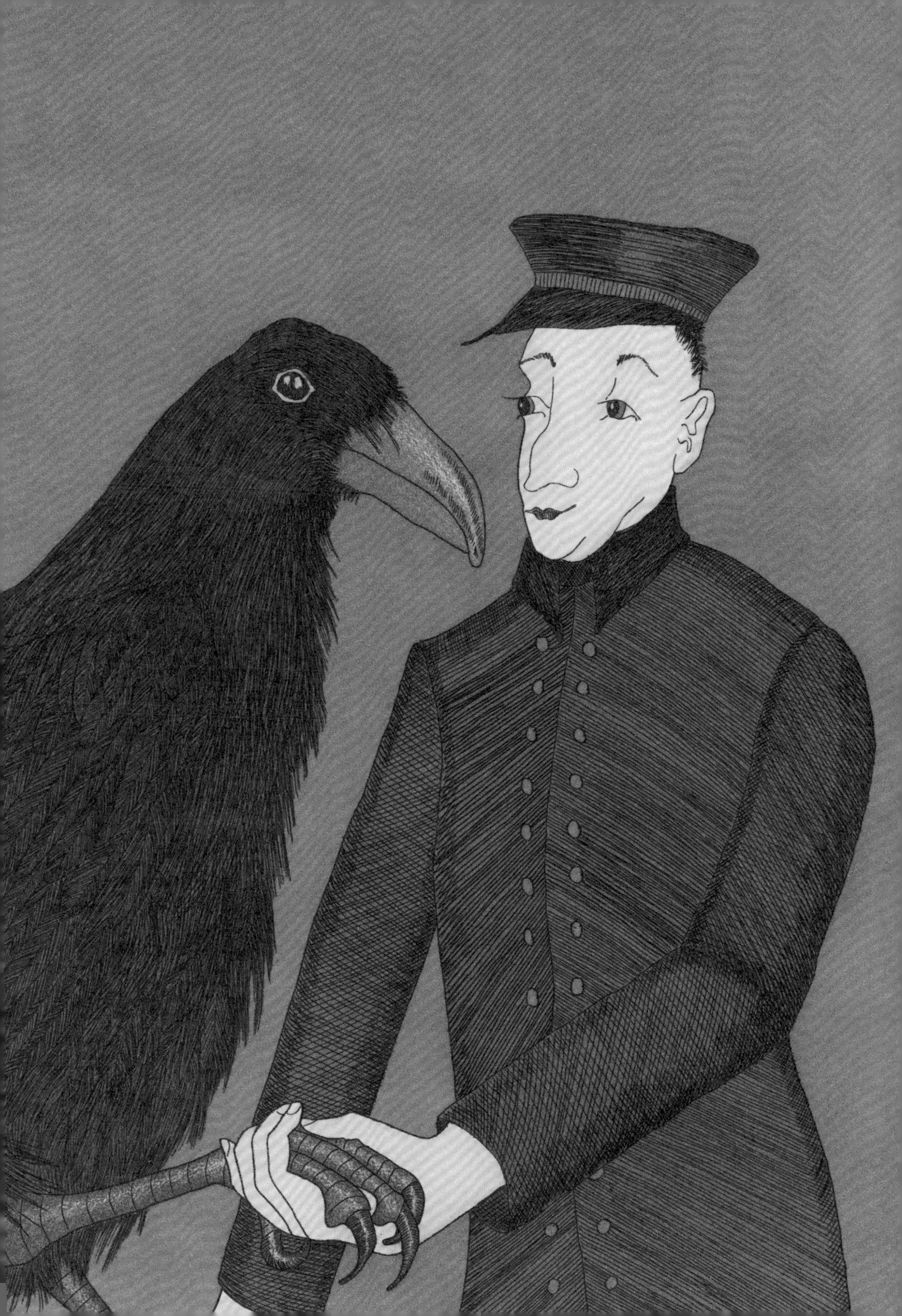

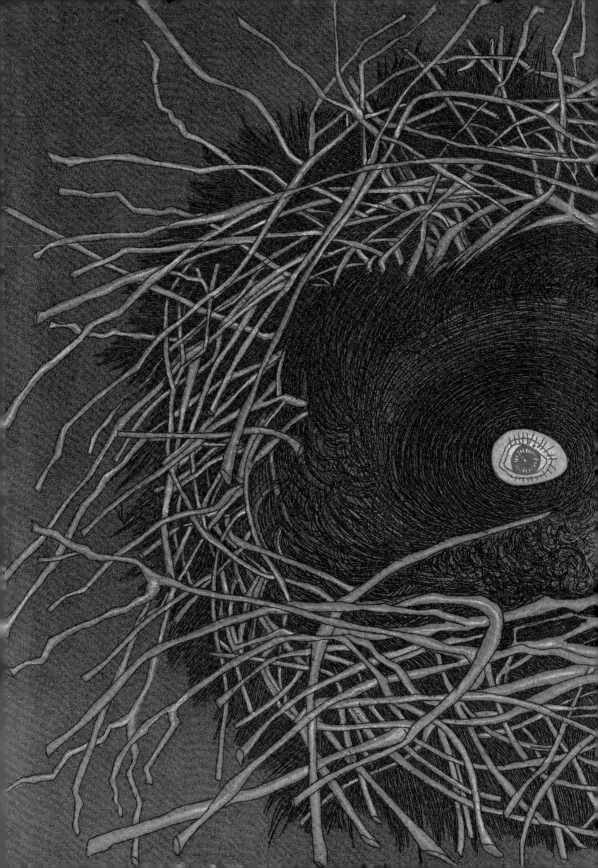

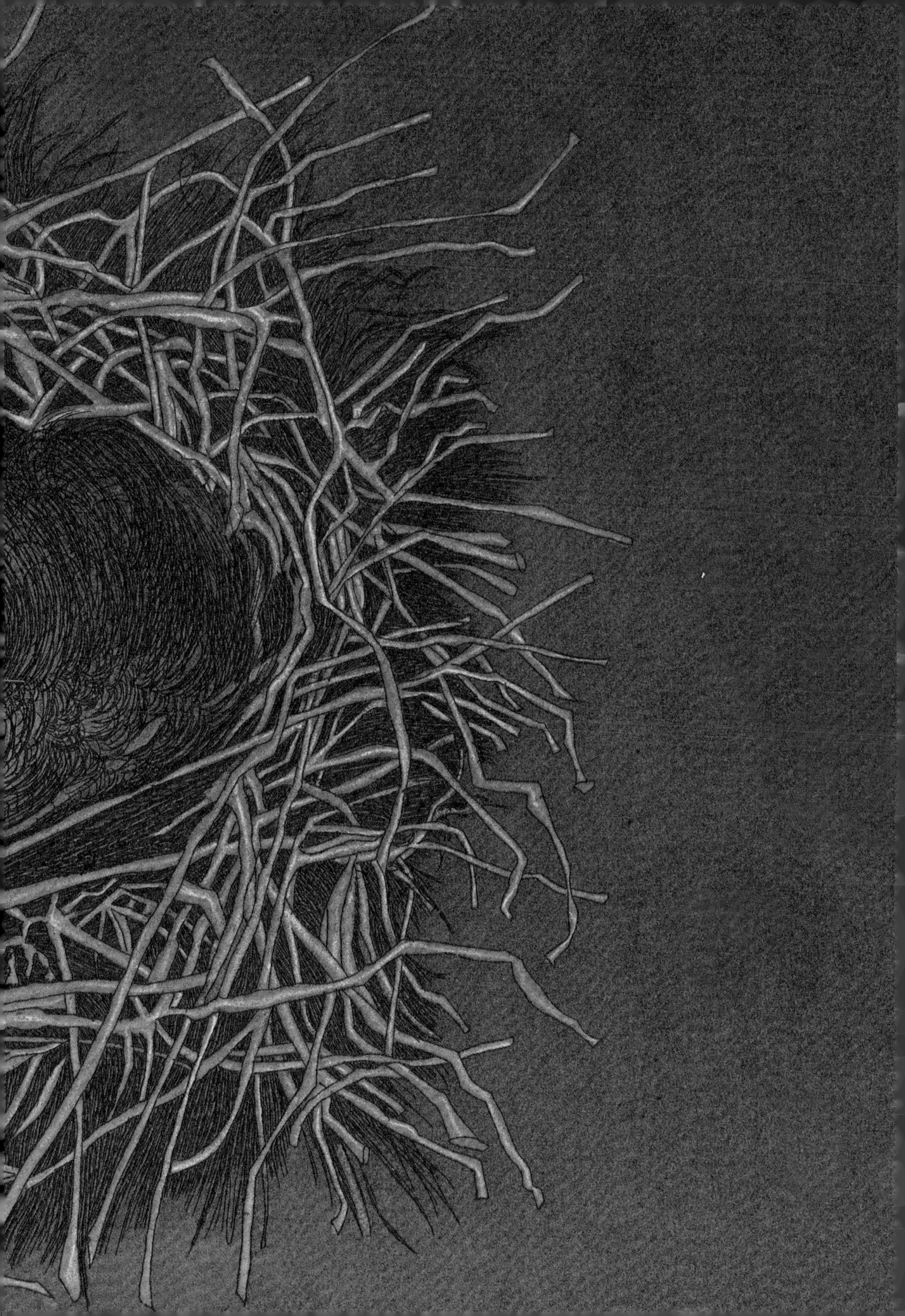

Then the egg was so big that the Raven kept sliding off it. The Postman worried that it wasn't warm enough, so he brought home hot-water bottles and woollen scarves for it. The egg kept growing. The Raven was confused. However, since she had never done this before, she just continued to incubate the massive egg.

Weeks went by, and then months. They could hear noises inside the egg, thumps and bumps. The expectant parents worried.

One morning the egg began to tremble. The creature inside it was beating against the eggshell. The parents stood waiting. The giant egg shook and rocked but did not break. "What if—?" said the Postman. "What if it doesn't have a beak?"

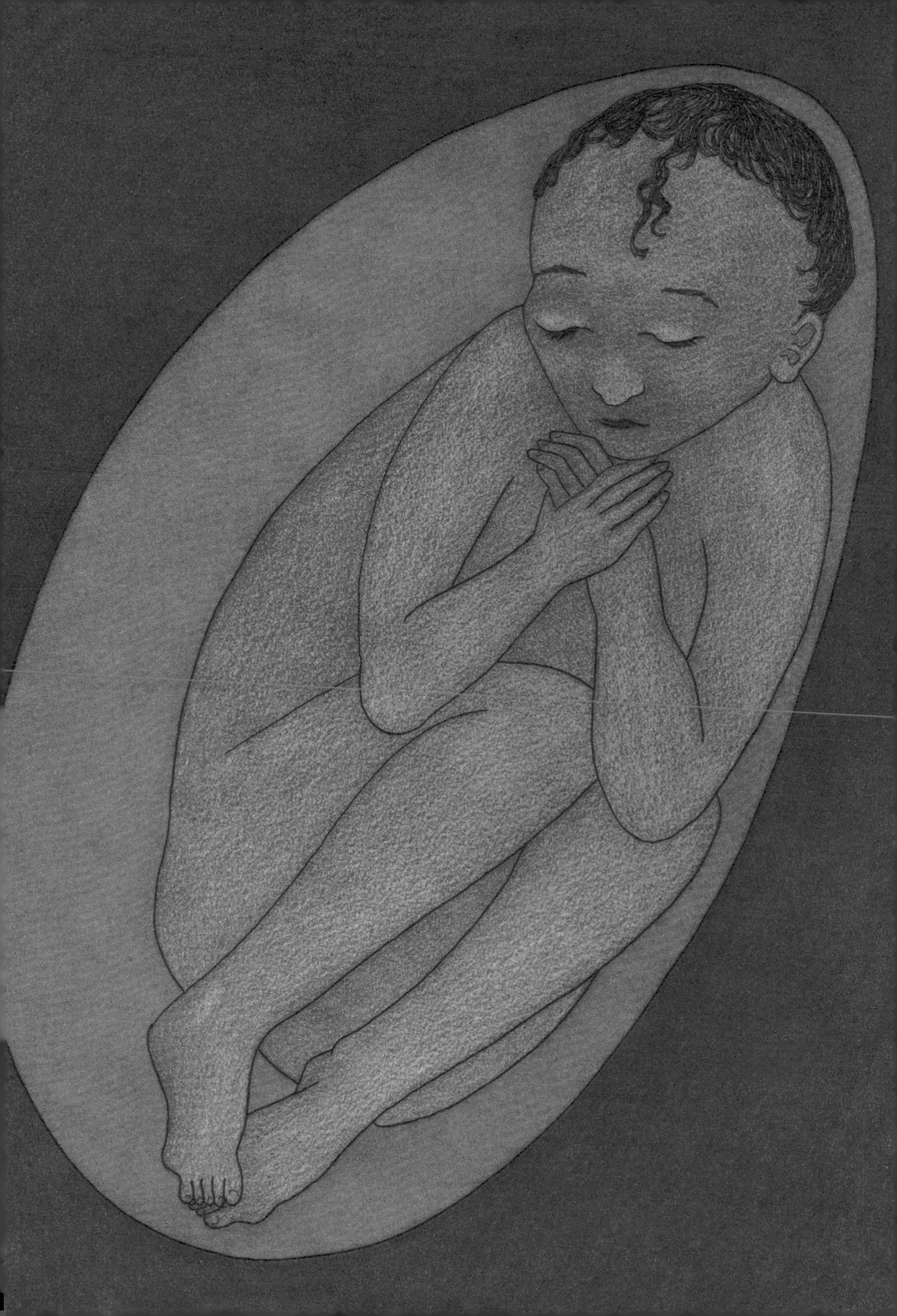

The Raven perched on top of the egg and chipped into it. She moved aside; the two of them waited. Out of the hole in the egg came two small hands.

The hands clutched at the eggshell and broke it away in pieces. Slowly, slowly, the arms, head, torso, and legs followed. It was a human girl.

She was small but perfectly formed. She had black hair and large dark eyes that gazed at the Raven and the Postman, unseeing. She lay gasping and exhausted on the kitchen table, soaked in fluid, silent. The Postman picked up the baby, held her upside down, and slapped her bottom. But instead of crying, the creature squawked. The Postman nearly dropped her, but recovered himself and placed her carefully on the table.

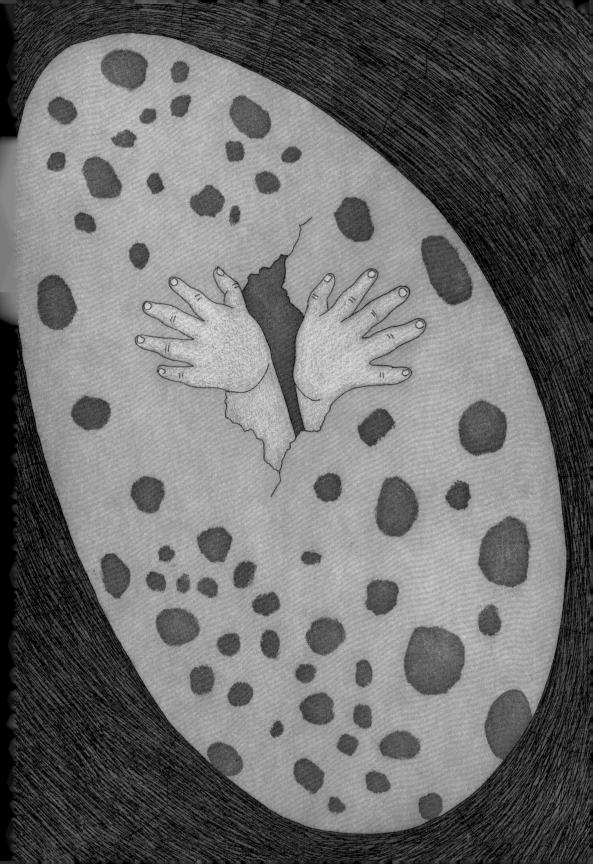

The Raven and the Postman stared at their daughter, unsure whether to be delighted or horrified.

———◆▸•◂◆———

The Raven Girl had a happy and perplexing childhood. She played odd games that involved hunting bugs and earthworms; she climbed trees and jumped out of them, hoping to fly but only crashing to the ground. She never spoke human words. All day long she sang and cawed, clicked and called.

"Why can't I fly?" she asked her mother, who understood her perfectly.

"You don't have wings, you have arms instead," replied the Raven. "Hands are a very fine thing to have; you should be glad."

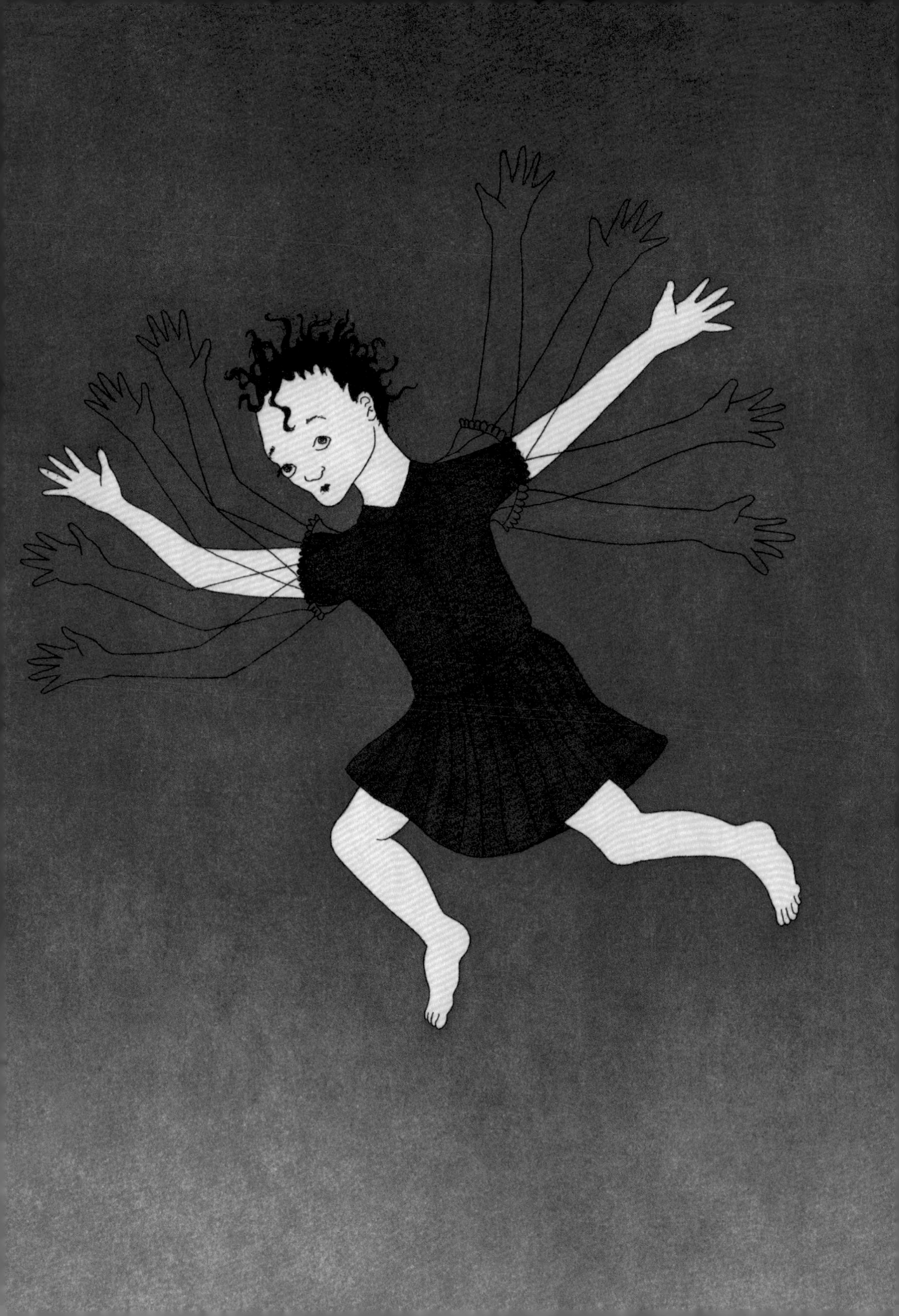

"I feel all wrong," the Raven Girl said. "I don't understand." She went outside and looked at the sky and felt quite desolate. The Postman saw her and picked her up. She held out her arms, and he raised her above his head. "Up, up!" she said, but he didn't understand.

————◆ ▶ ◆ ◀ ◆————

ne day the Raven Girl sat in the back garden reading a book. It was a hot summer day, and she was bored. A large black tomcat slunk under the fence and walked across the garden.

"Begone, Cat!" said the Raven Girl. Her mother had told her all about cats.

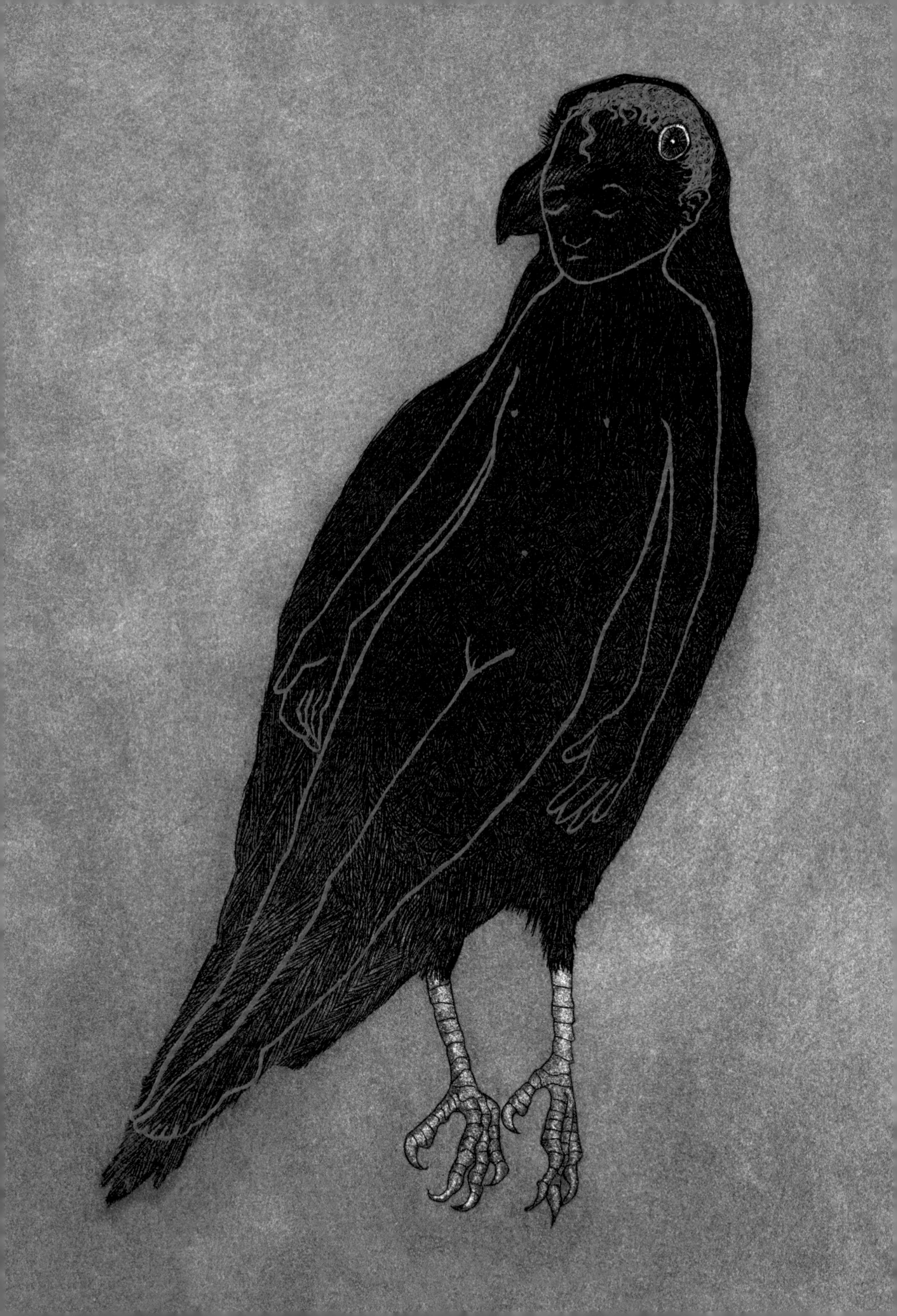

The Cat stopped and looked at her. "How is it that you happen to speak Raven?" he asked politely.

"My mother is a raven," the Raven Girl said.

"And your father?"

"My father is a postman."

"Of course," said the Cat. He bowed and left the garden the same way he had come.

The next day the Cat paid a call at the Court of the Ravens. He told the assembled Majesties about the Raven Girl. They listened patiently. The Cat concluded, "Perhaps she is the daughter of the young raven who disappeared?" The Majesties said they would look into it and thanked the Cat for his trouble. When he had gone they shook their heads at the absurdity of such a thing. Those cats!

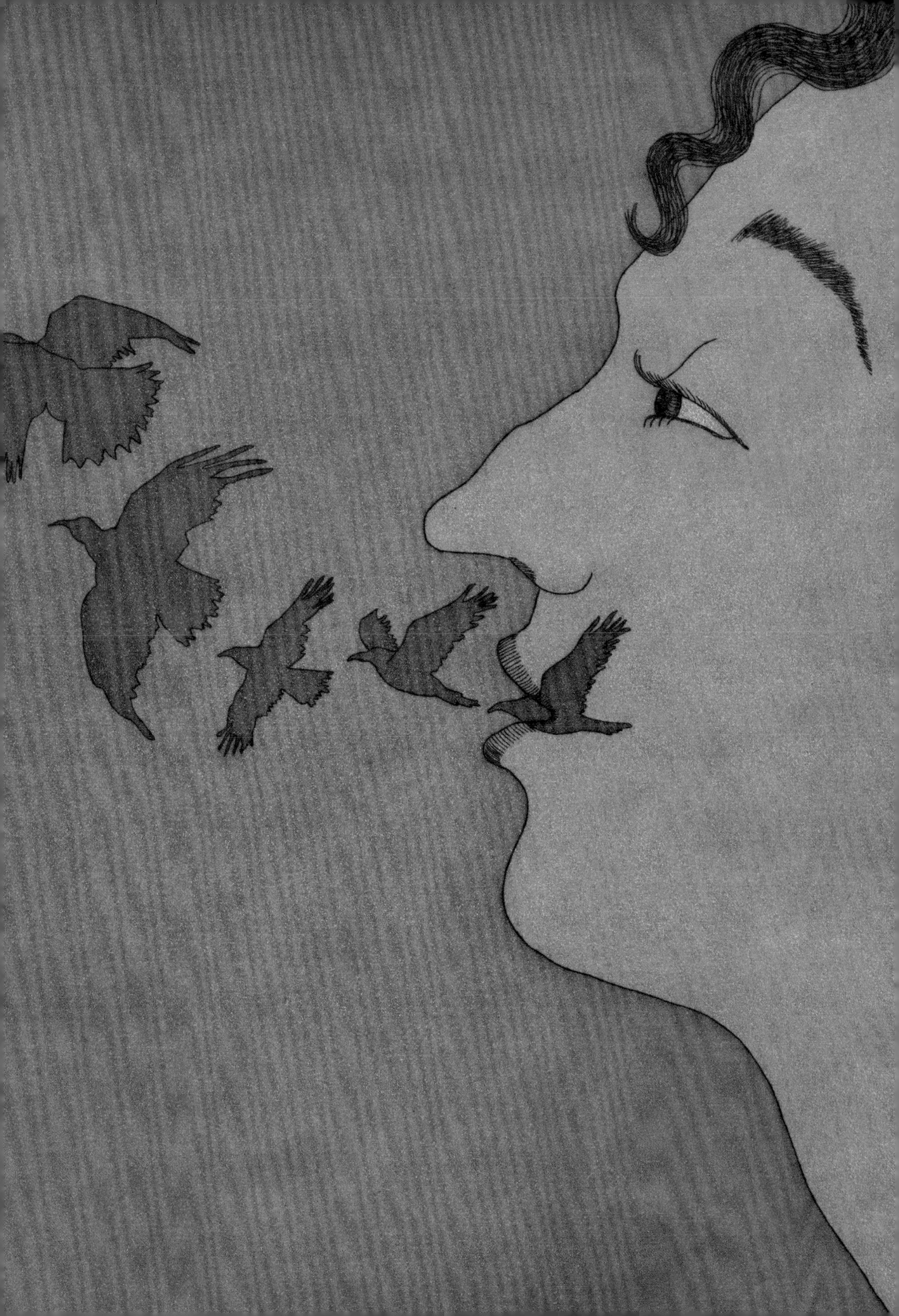

he Raven Girl went to school, but she never quite fit in with the other children. Instead of speaking, she wrote notes; when she laughed she made a harsh sound that startled even the teachers. The games the children played did not make sense to her, and no one wanted to play at flying or nest building or road kill for very long.

Years passed, and the Raven Girl grew. Her parents worried about her; no boys asked her out, she had no friends. Eventually it was time for the Raven Girl to make her own way in the world. The Postman told the University Admissions Board that his daughter was mute, and they replied that there were all sorts of special scholarships for the disabled, and that was that. The Postman and the Raven took the train into the city with their daughter; they helped her settle into her dorm room, took her out to a sumptuous lunch, and returned to their small house feeling very melancholy to find an actual empty nest sitting on the kitchen table, reminding them of happy times past.

———————◆▸▸◆◂◂◆———————

A t university everyone ignored the Raven Girl. She was so silent and shy that she was overlooked by the busy professors and students. They were large, larger than her dad even, and they looked right over the Raven Girl toward wherever they were going so quickly. The birds in the city were wary of her; she spoke in Raven to them, and they always looked surprised and flew away, as though she meant to trick them or eat them.

She was lonely. Her dorm room felt alien and rectangular, and her loud, enormous roommate was mostly out partying. The Raven Girl built herself a nest

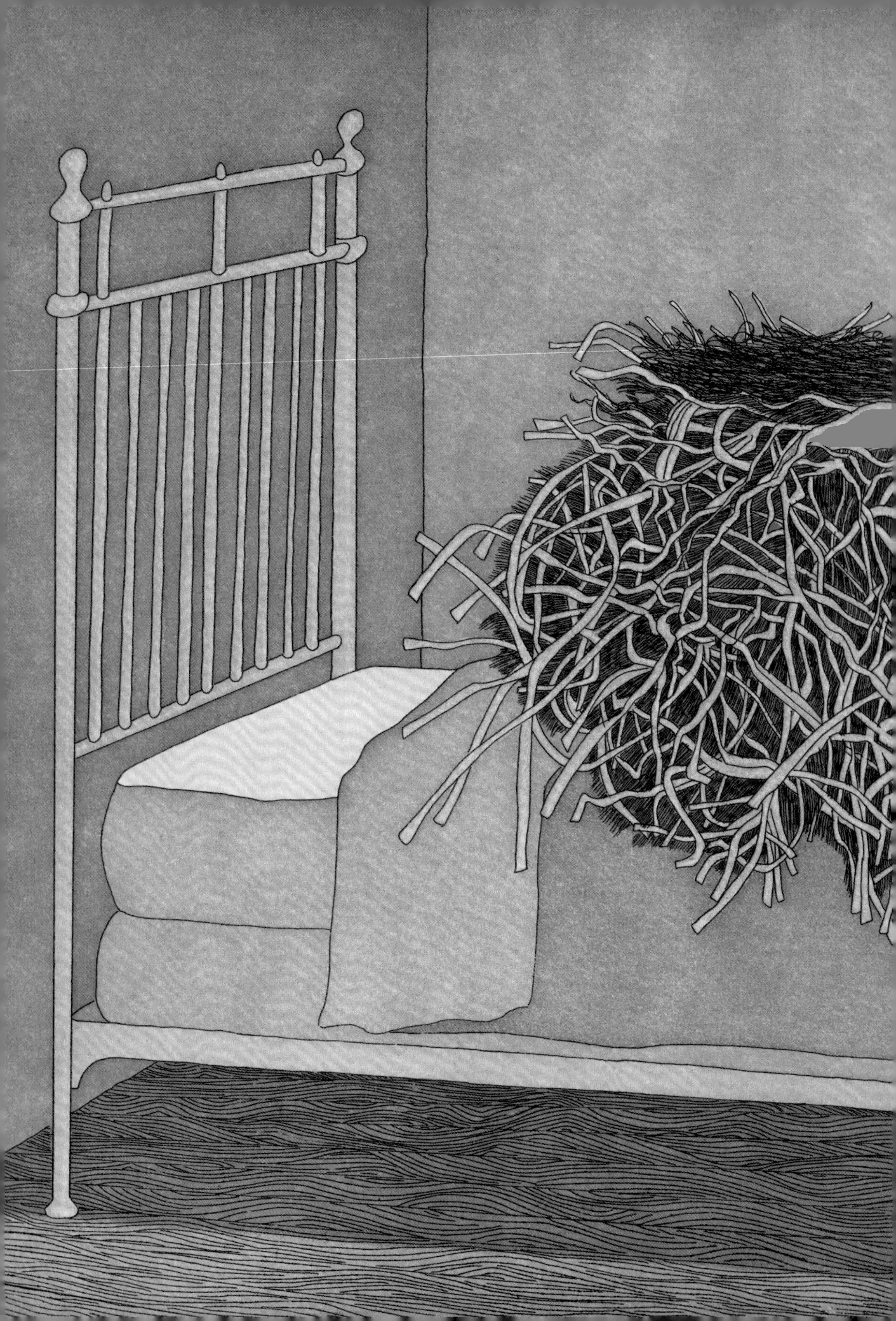

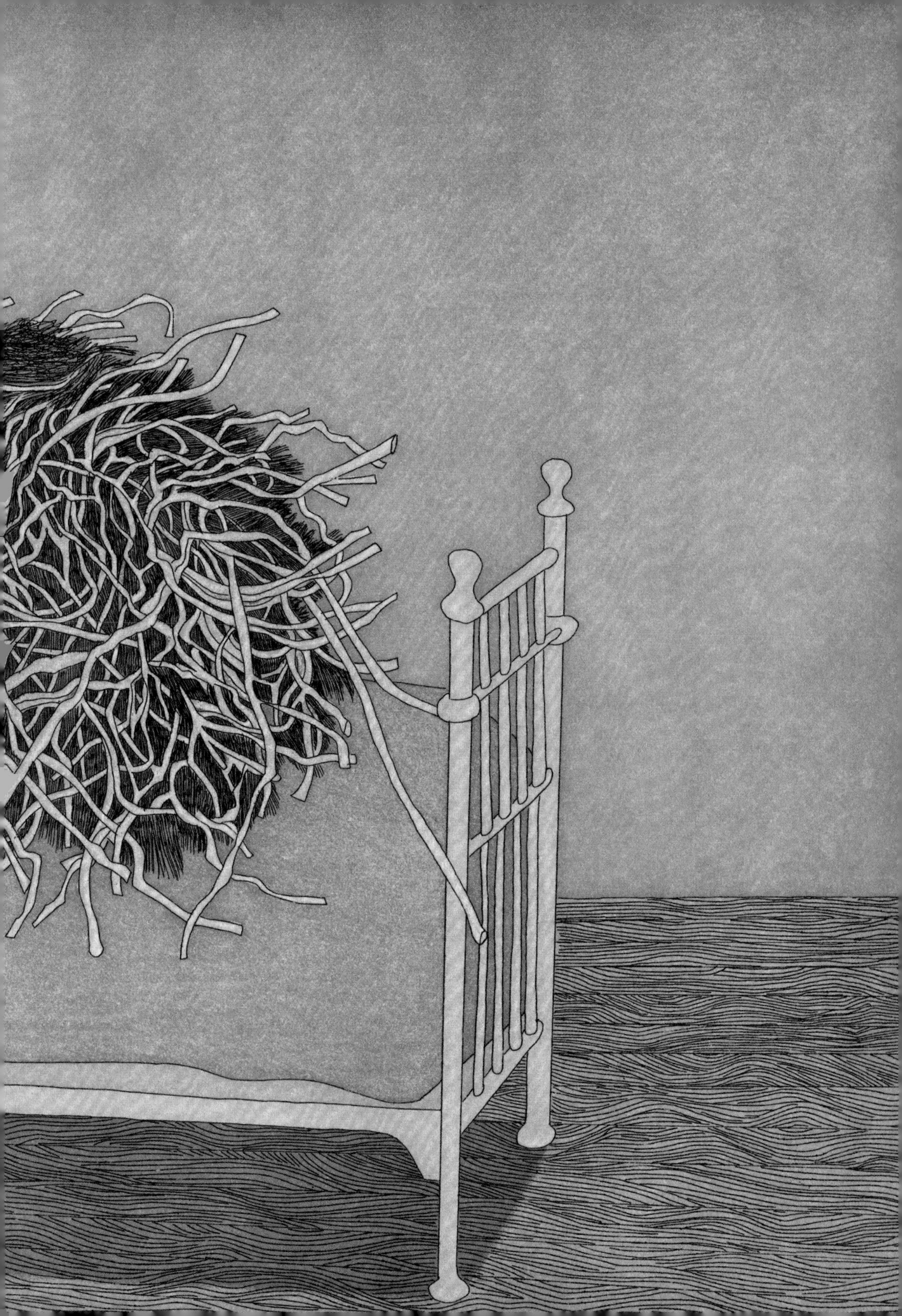

on top of her bed. Her roommate thought she was weird. She went to her classes and wrote her papers, but she made no friends.

Her room was on the top floor of a tall, hideous concrete building. *It looks like a prison,* she thought, though she had seen prisons only on TV. She opened the window and leaned out over the ledge. She was happy to be up high, and she took to climbing onto the ledge every evening to watch the sun setting. The lights would come on in the city then, and she would remind herself that the city had its own beauty, that she just had to learn to see it. She longed to push herself off the ledge, to lean forward and catch the night breeze under enormous black wings. Instead, she crawled back through the window and did her biology homework.

Though she felt utterly invisible, the Raven Girl had been noticed by someone. A boy in her biology class, who sat a few rows behind her, watched her and wondered about her. He was a shy boy, pale-skinned and dark-eyed. His hair was always falling in his face; he peered out at the Raven Girl and wondered if she was as shy as he was. She never spoke, but always looked alert and tilted her head when something interested her. The Boy imagined what he might say to her, what she might reply. He dreamed about her, puzzling dreams in which she spoke to him in a strange language that sounded like bird calls. But he never mustered the nerve to speak to her.

The biology class met in an old classroom, the seats arranged in steep tiers around the lecture platform. The walls were covered in ancient, inaccurate charts of the human brain, muscular system, and digestive tract, along with some pretty lithographs of fungus and the stages of primate evolution. The Raven Girl liked the professor, a woolly gentleman with innumerable corduroy jackets who lectured to the class about cell structure and genetics.

One morning she arrived at class to find that they were having a visiting lecturer. He looked fairly ordinary: middle-aged, balding, bespectacled, and perhaps a bit pleased with himself. He blinked a lot. The professor introduced this person to the class, reading a list of honours and papers and degrees; he was a doctor, a plastic surgeon. The students wondered what a plastic surgeon was doing in their evolutionary biology class.

"Chimeras," announced the Doctor. "Today we are going to talk about where the human race may be headed. We have the power to improve ourselves, if we wish to do so. We can become anything we wish to be. Behold."

The room darkened, and moving images filled the screen behind the podium. A man with a forked lizard tongue. A woman with horns. A man with long claws. A man with cat eyes. A woman with extra thumbs. A woman with a prehensile tail. A man whose hands opened like a Swiss army knife, full of hardware. A woman with fangs. A woman with enormous white wings, like an angel.

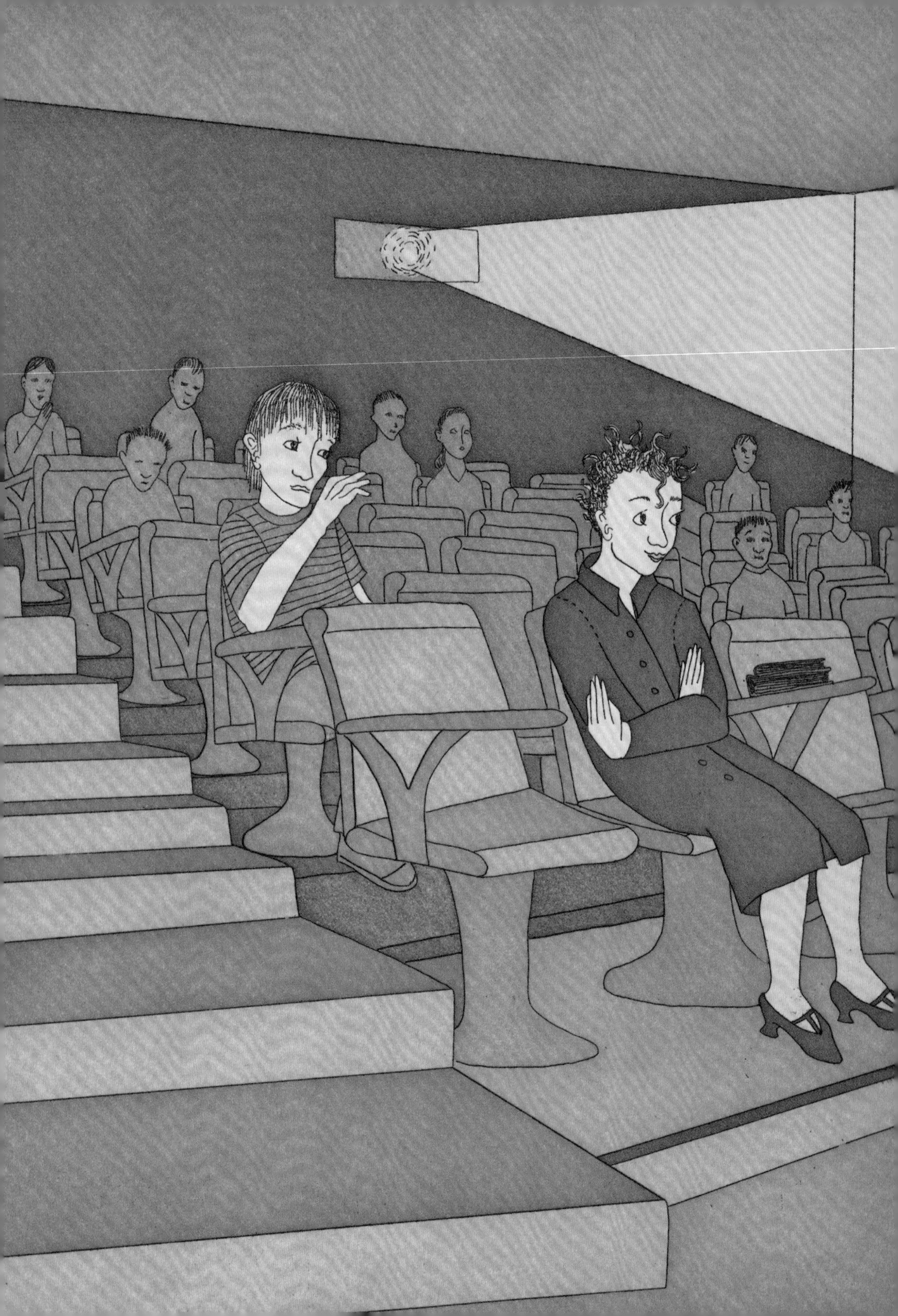

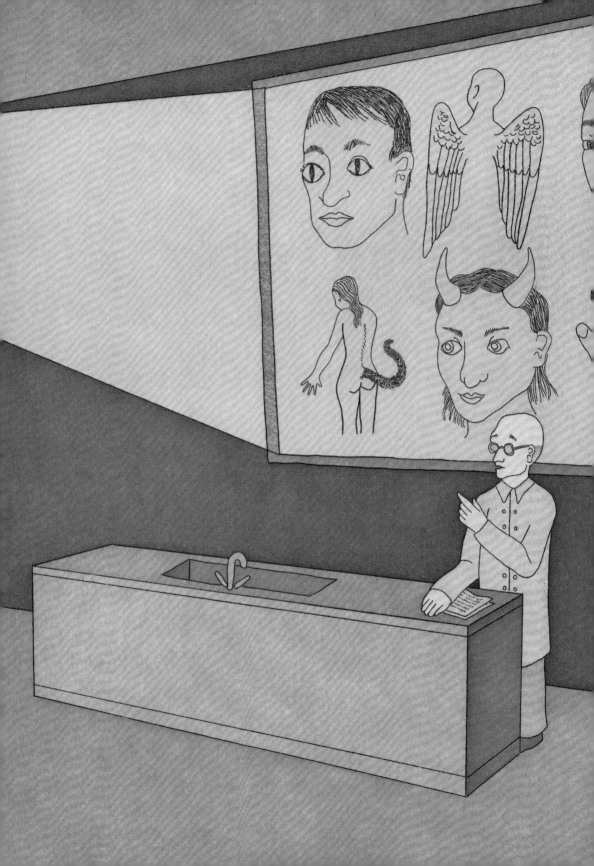

The Raven Girl stood up. She had urgent questions, but she had forgotten that she had no human words. "Yes?" said the Doctor. She opened her mouth to speak, then shook her head, sat down again. The Professor whispered to the Doctor, who glanced curiously at the Raven Girl. She blushed.

The class bristled with questions for the Doctor. *How could this be ethical? Wasn't it frivolous to spend so much time and money making ourselves nonhuman, or superhuman? What about poor people, shouldn't they be able to improve themselves too? Was this art, or science? What about God? If we were made in his image...?*

The Raven Girl listened carefully and took notes. But her questions were quite different. The class ended; the students filed out. The Raven Girl hesitated. The Boy kept his seat, waiting to see what she would do. She approached the Doctor, who was gathering his notes and chatting to the Professor. She handed him a note.

Can you make me into a bird?

The Doctor looked at her carefully, kindly.

"Why do you want to do that?" he asked.

She wrote: *My mother is a raven and my father is a postman, but I feel that truly I should have been a raven.*

"Come to my office on Wednesday," said the Doctor. "We'll talk about it then."

The Raven Girl smiled. She left the classroom feeling hopeful. The Boy followed her, but she didn't notice him.

Wednesday arrived. The Raven Girl came into the Doctor's office to find him sitting behind his desk working at his computer amidst piles of papers and books. He beamed at her.

"Have a seat. By the way, how old are you? Do your parents know you're here?"

18, she wrote in her notebook. *No.*

"Hmm," he said. "Well, you're old enough to decide for yourself, but you are awfully young to be doing something so permanent. And so unusual."

Will I be able to fly? she wrote.

The Doctor looked startled. "No," he said. "Birds have hollow bones, they weigh almost nothing. You are too heavy to fly."

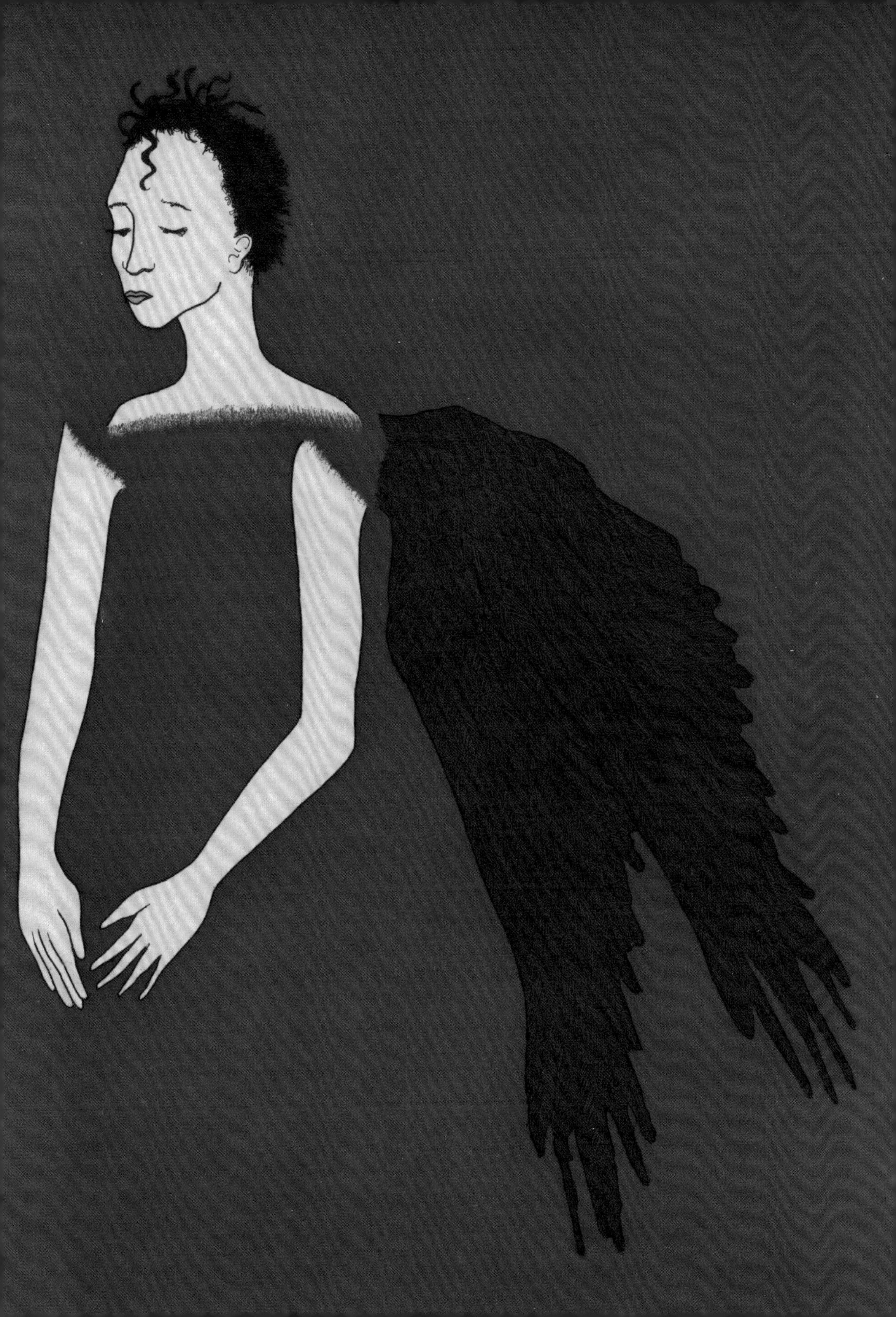

The Raven Girl raised her arms, the way she had always done for her father when she wanted to be picked up. The Doctor hesitated, then lifted her. She weighed almost nothing; her bones were hollow.

Inside I am a raven, she wrote. *I only look human.*

"Birds' wings are their arms," said the Doctor. "If you want to fly, your arms must become your wings."

Yes, she wrote. *Make my arms into wings, please.*

The Doctor was troubled. "I don't know if I can do this," he said. "Most of the things I do for people are aesthetic, not functional. It might not work. You might have wings and still not be able to fly."

Let's try, she wrote. *Please.*

They stared at each other, the Doctor unsure, the Raven Girl beseeching. "Please," she said in her raven language. "Please help me." She bowed her head and opened her hands to him, supplicant.

"I'll try," he said.

———— ❧ ————

The hospital was enormous, ugly, and not very new. The Raven Girl had a room to herself on the top floor. She could see her dorm room a few blocks away. The city bustled beneath her as she leaned out the big window. The first day she came there, the Doctor sat down with her and opened his laptop.

"This is how we will make you into a bird," he said.

The images showed the structure of a raven's various feathers, the structure of a raven's wing. The similarities between wing bones and arm bones. How the wing might attach to her shoulder; the muscles and tendons that must serve new purposes. The stem cells that must be reprogrammed to grow wings rather than arms. The sequence of the surgeries: amputations, attachments. Neurons must be trained to fire, nerves must be rerouted. The brain must recognize the new wings, the immune system must not reject them.

"Then you will have wings," said the Doctor.

And then, will I fly? she wrote.

"Maybe," he said.

———✦✦·✦✦———

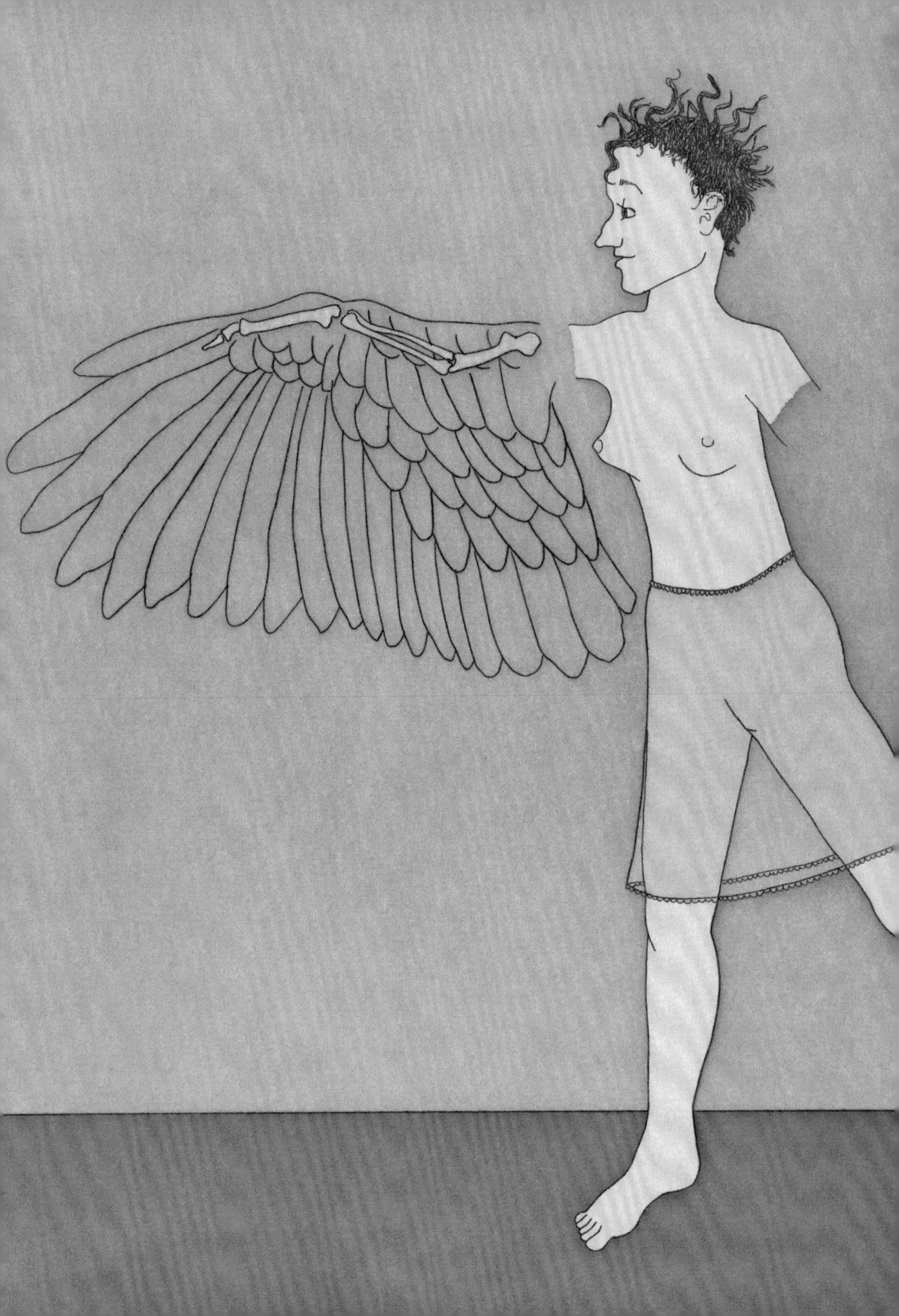

The Boy didn't understand. The Raven Girl did not come to class anymore. He went to her dorm room and waited for her, but she never came there. He wondered if he should tell someone. He wondered who her parents were, where they lived. Had she dropped out of school, gone home? The Boy was sad. Though he didn't know anything about her, he longed for the Raven Girl. Where was she? He decided to investigate. He would become the Boy Detective.

He spied on her roommate. He hacked into the Raven Girl's e-mail and found out where her parents lived. Something was very peculiar, but he could not pin it down. At night he had odd dreams. *He went to the movies with an enormous black bird. She ate popcorn. He put his arm around her shoulders, then he was not sure if*

birds have shoulders. The movie was Hitchcock's The Birds.
*Then the birds came off the screen and flew around inside
the theatre.* He woke up sweating. The Boy Detective
resolved to find the Raven Girl, no matter what.
Something bad had happened to her, he just knew it.

---

our wings are ready," said the Doctor. He
led the Raven Girl into his laboratory.
It was full of tanks and jars, each one
an artificial womb nurturing a limb,
organ, or animal. The lab was filled with
beautiful blue light. The Raven Girl
stood in the middle of the room with her hands
over her eyes. The Doctor wheeled in an enormous
tank and halted it before her. "Ta da!" he said. She
opened her eyes.

The wings were black, perfect, huge. The Raven Girl pressed her nose against the glass of the tank. Tubes fed the wings, liquid bubbled around them.

"What do you think?" the Doctor asked. She threw her arms around him, overcome with delight.

The Boy Detective had tracked her down. He had followed many false clues over weeks of lonely vigilance, but here she was, at last. He stood in the doorway of her hospital room, watching her. The Raven Girl was leaning out the window, her back to him.

"Hello?" he said.

She turned away from the window. The room was in shadow, she was a silhouette. There was

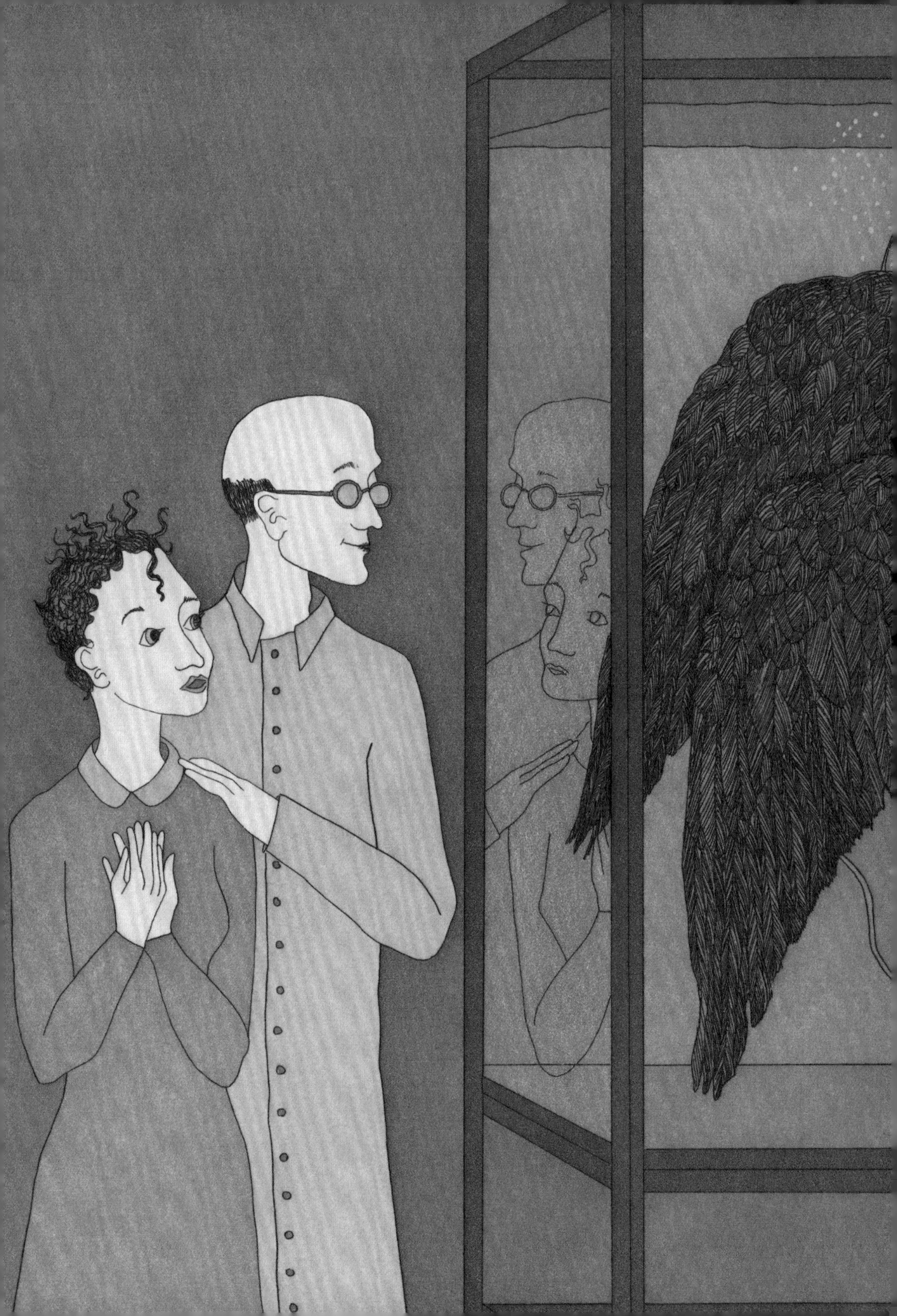

something not right about her shape. She stood with her head tilted inquisitively, waiting.

"I'm from your biology class," he said. "I noticed you stopped coming. Are you okay?" He stepped toward her. She stepped backwards. "Sometimes I dream about you."

A deep voice behind him said, "And how is my little ravenette today?" The Doctor stepped into the room and flicked on the lights. The Boy Detective suddenly saw what had eluded him about her figure: The Raven Girl had no arms. A skein of tubes emanated from her arm sockets, blood coursing through them and back into her body.

The Boy Detective turned and ran. His footsteps echoed from the hall, and became fainter as he clattered down the stairs.

"Who was that?" the Doctor asked the Raven Girl. She shrugged: *Does it matter?* The Doctor stood and listened, but the Boy Detective did not return. "Oh, well," said the Doctor. "Let's have a look at those dressings. How are you feeling?" The Raven Girl smiled. The Doctor felt a pang of misgiving, but he smiled back at her anyway.

———— ◆ ◆ ◆ ◆ ————

The next morning the Raven Girl woke up early. Nurses came and prepped her for surgery. She lay on a gurney and sang to herself as they wheeled her down the long hallway. She saw the wings waiting for her in the operating room, bubbles rising around them in their big tank. The

Doctor said her name. Then the anaesthesia kicked in and her world went dark.

———◄►◄►———

She woke up swathed in bandages, unable to move. "Hush," said the Doctor. "Go back to sleep." The Nurse gave her an injection, and she stumbled into a dream. *She was flying. The world was toy-like below her. She saw her house; her father stood in the garden, waving. Her mother was flying beside her. Then they were surrounded by ravens, all flying together, a sky of black wings.* When she woke again she could hear birds singing outside her window.

———◄►◄►———

eeks later, the nurses removed the bandages. The Raven Girl thought, *It's like coming out of the egg. But what will be born this time?*

The Raven Girl stood before the long mirror. She turned this way, that way, marvelling. The black wings seemed to have always been there, so perfectly did they emerge from her shoulders. It was as though a secret part of her had been made visible. She tried to move them and winced. There were still bruises. The Doctor stood behind her, watching. "Don't worry," he said. "It will get easier. You have to practise."

She practised. Every day she was a little stronger. The wings began to obey her mind. She fluttered and flapped, took little running leaps, and rose a few feet into the air. She felt like a child again, playing at flying. But perhaps she was a fledgling now, and if she practised she must eventually fly? The Doctor worried about her. She tried to be cheerful for him.

Then one morning her parents arrived. The Boy Detective was with them.

The Raven Girl ran to her parents. They embraced her carefully. She stretched out her wings and rotated slowly for them, smiling.

"Wow," said the Postman.

"But, darling——," said the Raven in her raven language.

"I'm going to fly!" their daughter told them.

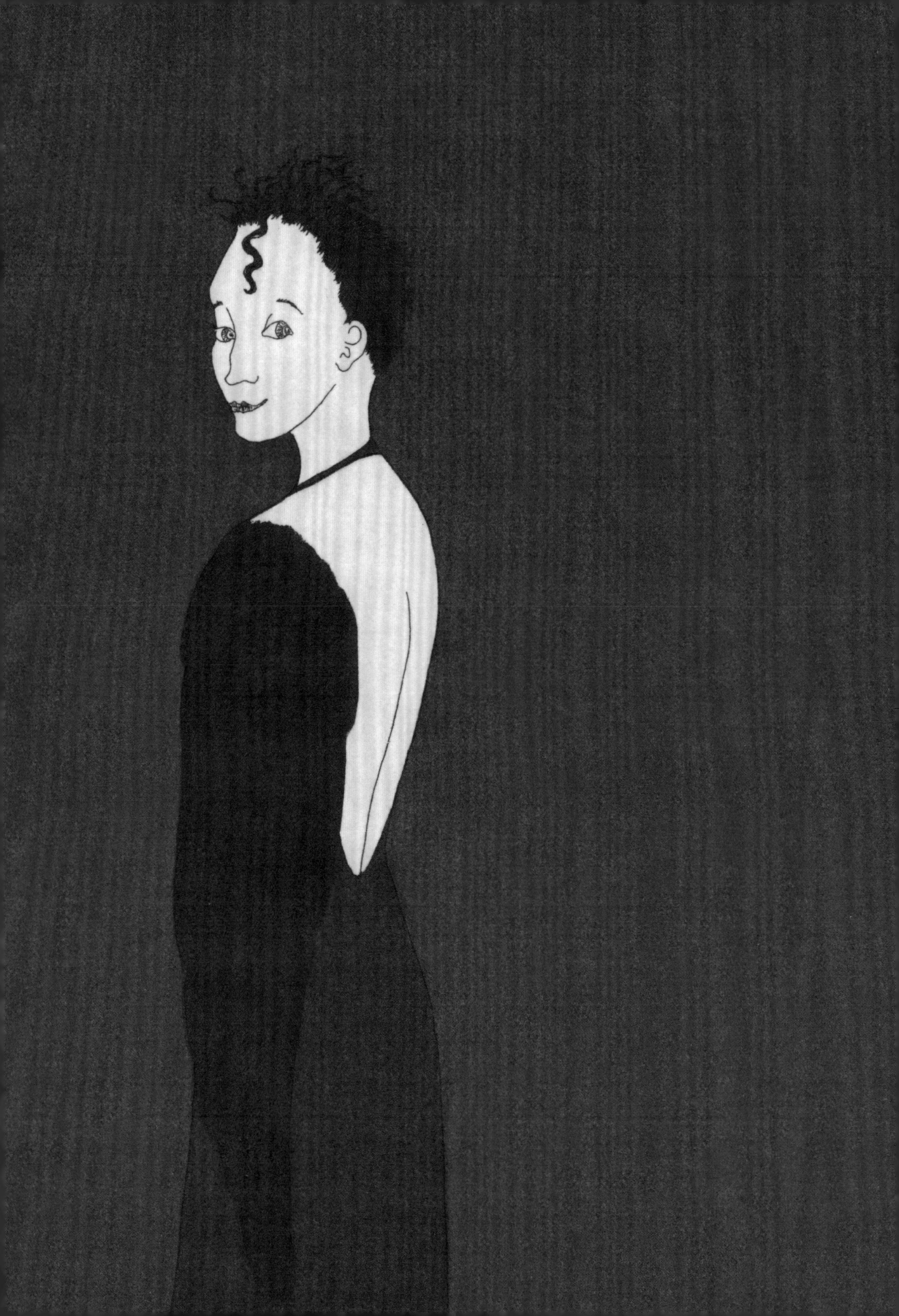

The Raven inclined her head uncertainly as the Doctor came into the room.

"That's him," said the Boy Detective. "He did this to her."

"Will it work?" asked the Postman. "Will she fly?"

"She's trying," the Doctor said. "We don't know yet. There's no reason she shouldn't be able to."

"This is illegal," said the Boy Detective. "Call the police!"

"Do you know this boy?" the Raven asked her daughter.

"I don't think so," said the Raven Girl. "But he keeps showing up and freaking out."

"Young man—," the Doctor began, but the Boy Detective interrupted him.

"You should be in jail! You should be shot! Why isn't anyone upset?" He turned to the Raven Girl. "Someone has to save you, and if they won't, I will!" He leapt forward and tried to grab her. She lurched away from him, and the Doctor and the Postman grabbed the Boy Detective. But he twisted free, and they all stood staring at each other, no one sure what to do next.

The Doctor pressed the call button by the bed. "Someone will be here in a minute," he said. "Why don't you just leave?"

The Boy Detective hesitated. He looked at the Raven Girl. She turned her head away abruptly. The Doctor said, "She doesn't want——," and the Boy Detective suddenly pummelled into him, propelled him across the room toward the open window, and though the Doctor screamed and struggled and clung to the sill, the Boy Detective pushed him out.

The Raven Girl ran to the window. The city spread before her; the Doctor's body was a small white speck on the hospital lawn. She jumped onto the windowsill. "No!" cried her parents. The Postman was wrestling with the Boy Detective, but he let him go and tried to grab the Raven Girl. She spread her wings and jumped.

At first she fell. She tried to think, *How does this work, what should I do?* Then she stopped thinking. Her raven body knew: Her wings spread out, the air caught her, and she began to fly.

She flew in spiralling circles, down and down, slowly and silently. She landed with an ungainly thump a little distance from the Doctor's body. People had gathered around it. The Raven Girl broke into the cluster. The Doctor lay broken, his spectacles glinting up at nothing. She threw her wings over him and laid her head on his chest and cried.

━━━▶▶◆◀◀━━━

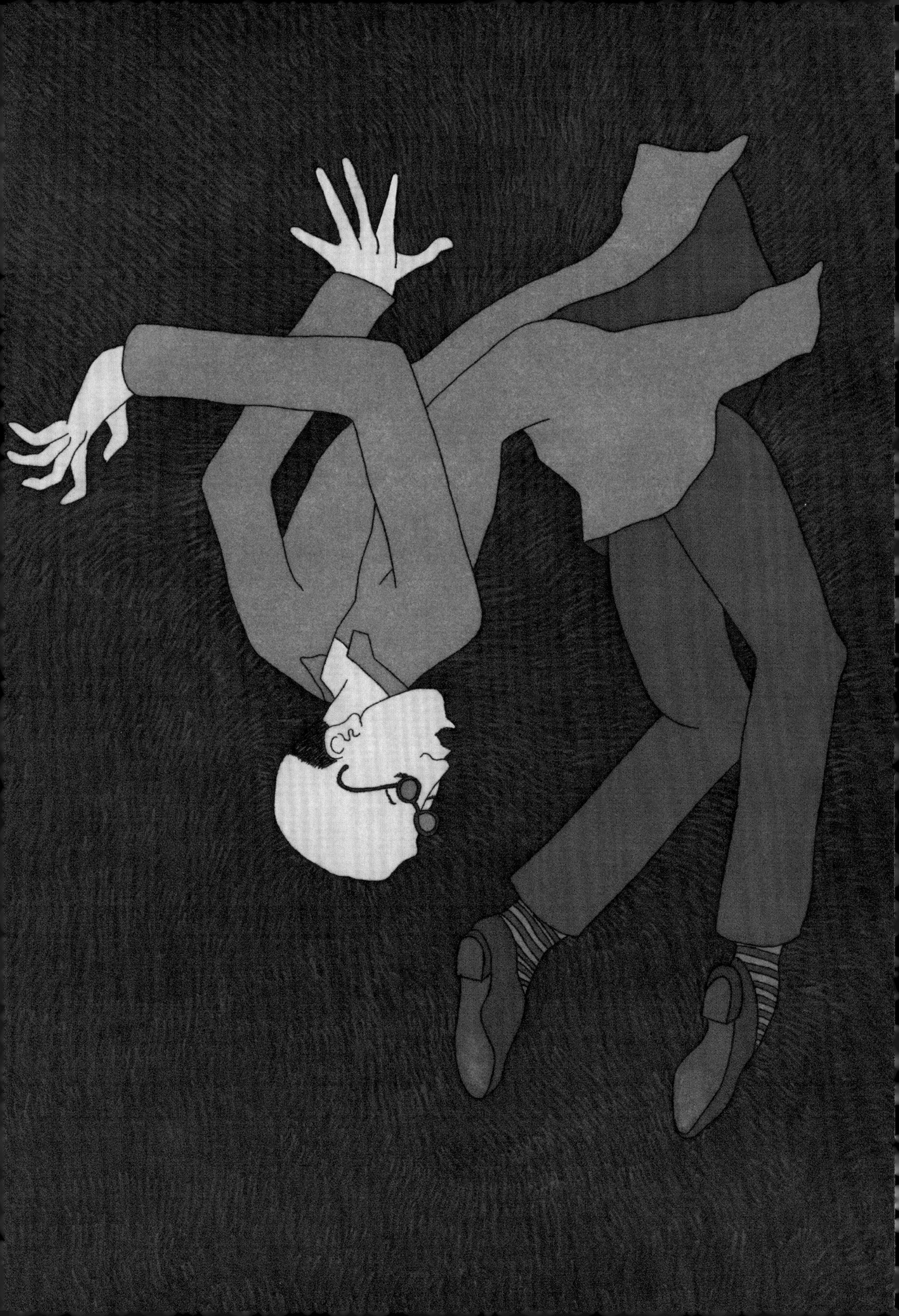

he Raven Girl did not go to the Doctor's funeral. She waited until all the mourners had left the cemetery and the gravediggers had finished their work. Then she crept softly to the new grave and placed a long black feather on the fresh mound of earth.

---

s for the Boy Detective, no one could find him. He had run out of the hospital room and disappeared into the confusion of the city. The police searched for weeks but gave up when all the leads went cold. The newspapers and the TV news ran his picture every day, but at last they lost interest. The Boy Detective had vanished.

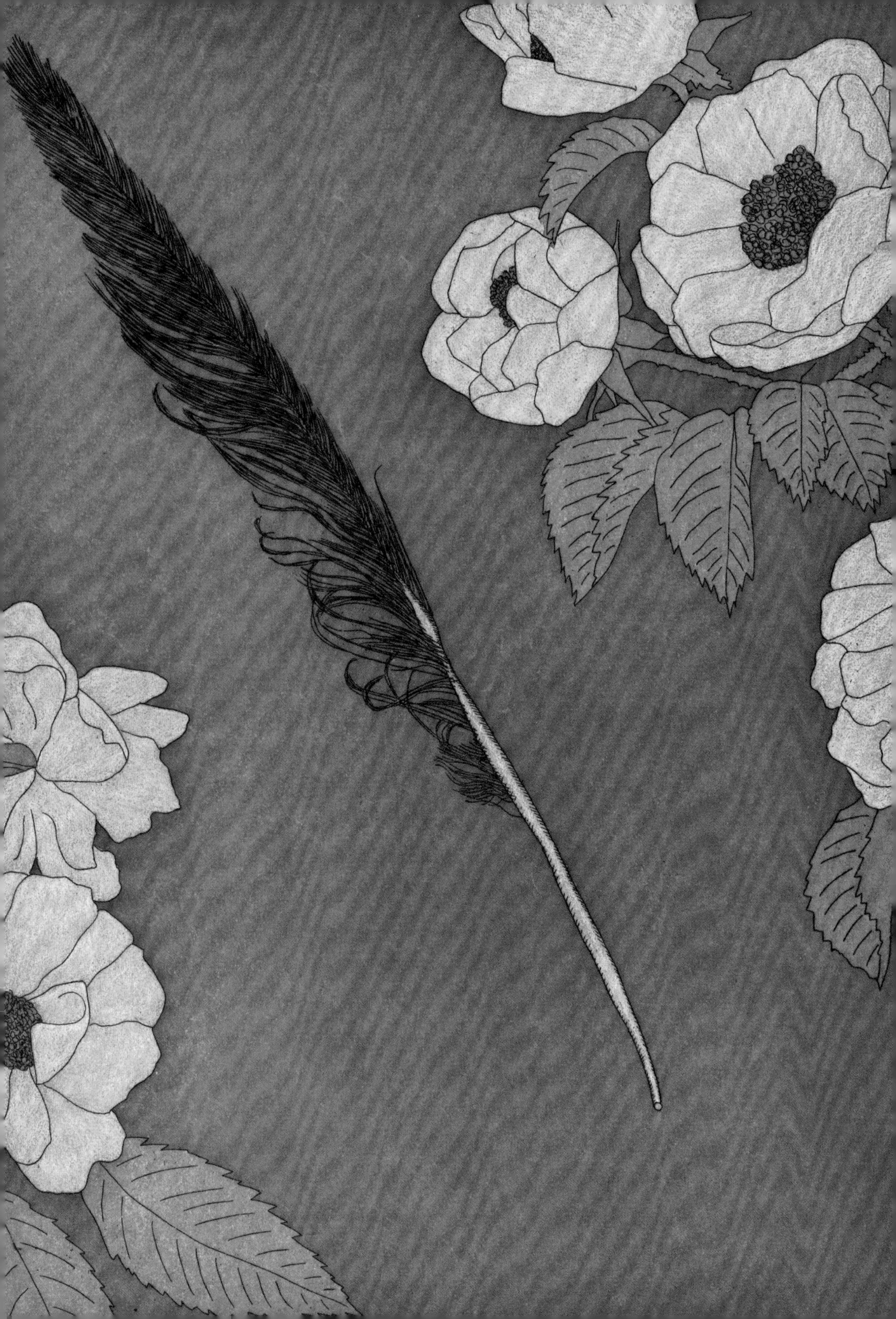

The Raven Girl, the Postman, and the Raven finally went home and tried to figure out what to do next. There were movie offers, and for a while the Raven Girl thought she might like to work for a circus. But nothing seemed quite right.

———— ◆▸◆◂◆ ————

In the flatlands by the cliffs out in East Underwhelm (East of East, Lower Heights) the Cat noticed someone walking alone. The Cat caught up with him and began to walk beside him.

"Hey puss," said the Boy Detective. The Cat, who was an avid reader of newspapers, swished his tail and did not reply. The Boy Detective shrugged and kept walking.

The Cat ran on ahead until he came to the Court of the Ravens. He showed the ravens a newspaper and told them the whole story. He tried not to be smug about it.

The ravens were indignant. They demanded action. The Majesties ordered an investigation. The Raven's family were elated to discover that their daughter was alive. The Cat didn't hang around. He was pleased to be taken seriously, though.

The Boy Detective wasn't sure where he was going. It had seemed like a good idea to get out of the city, but now he was lost. The land was quite empty, and he had run out of sandwiches.

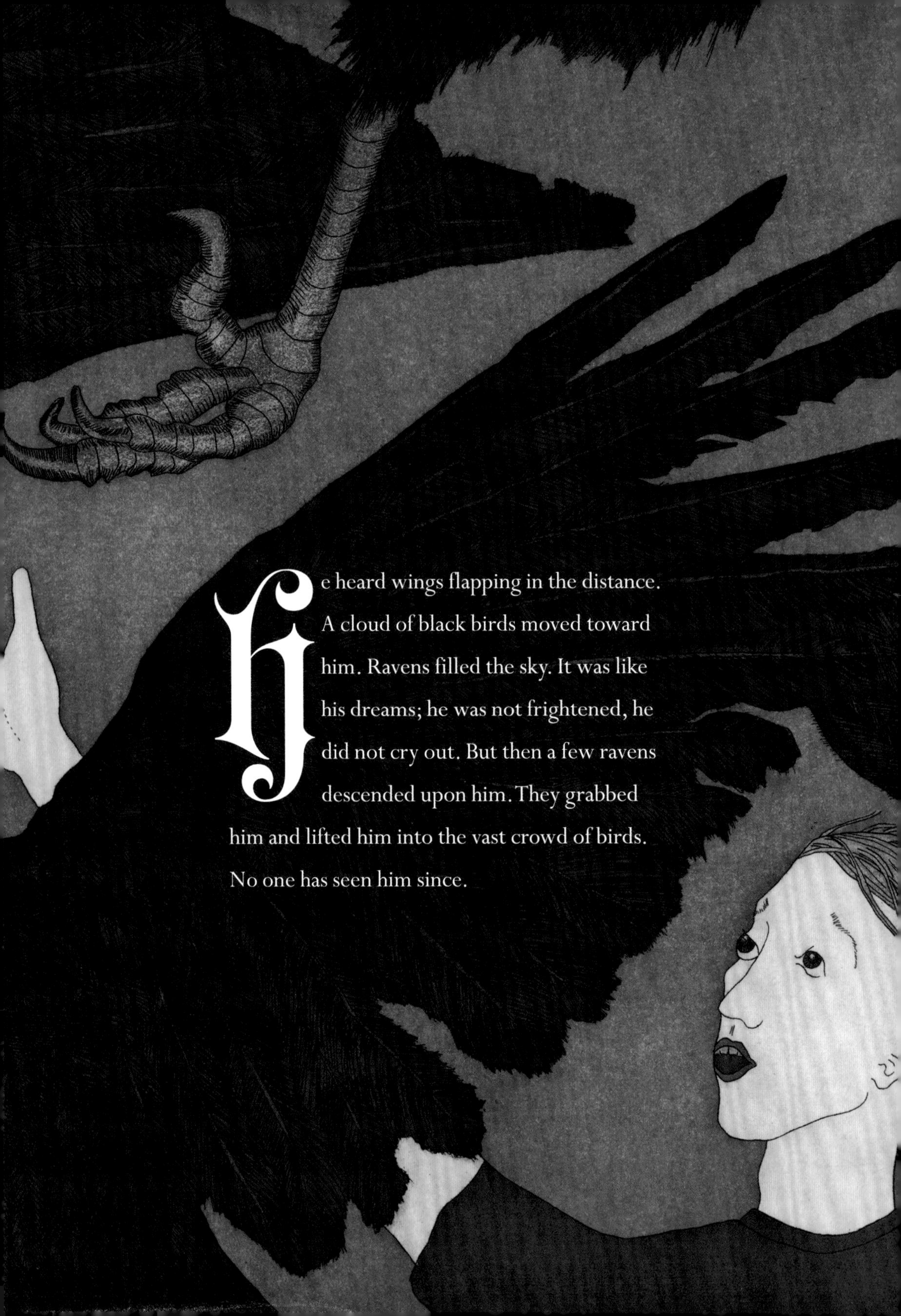

He heard wings flapping in the distance. A cloud of black birds moved toward him. Ravens filled the sky. It was like his dreams; he was not frightened, he did not cry out. But then a few ravens descended upon him. They grabbed him and lifted him into the vast crowd of birds. No one has seen him since.

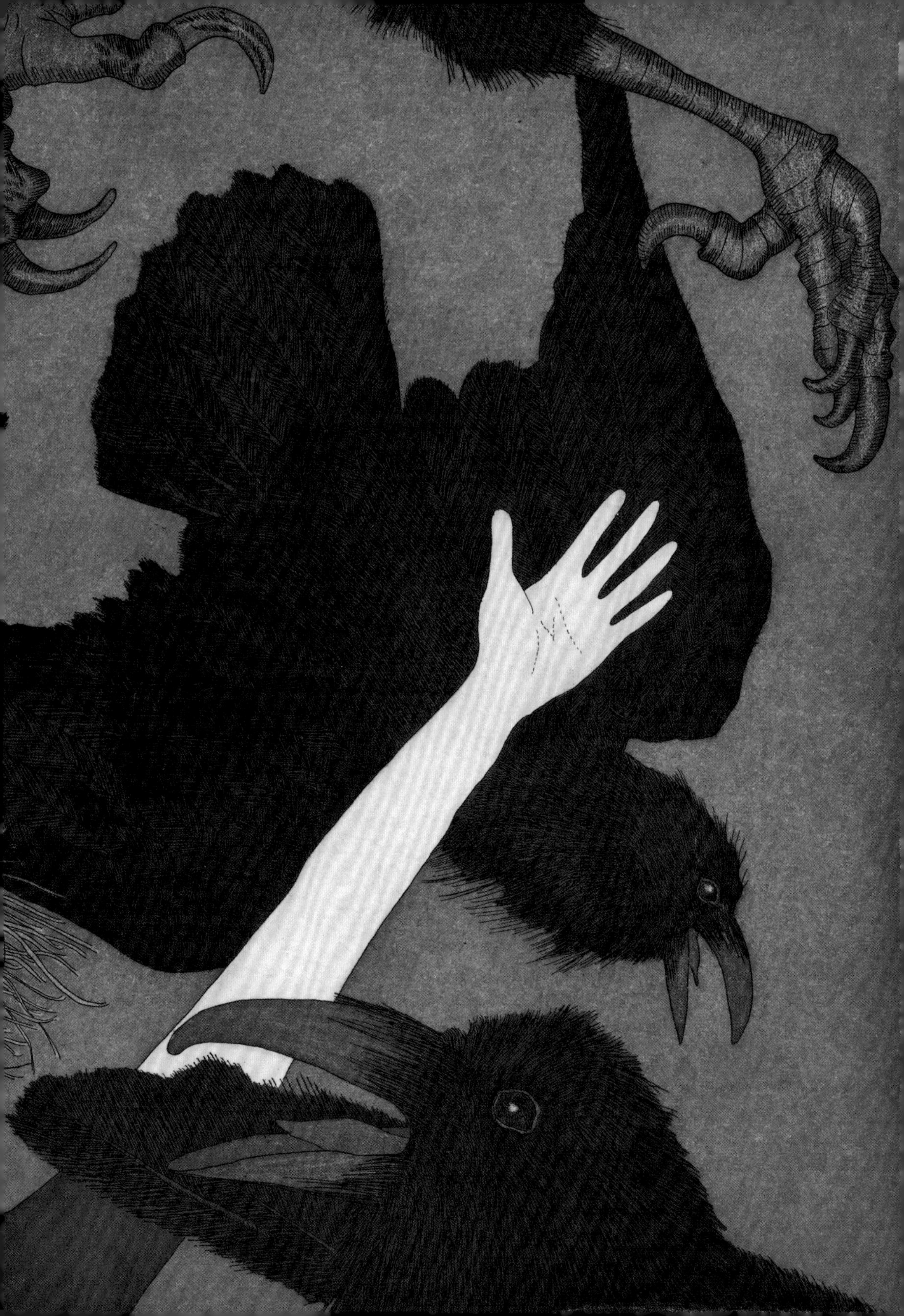

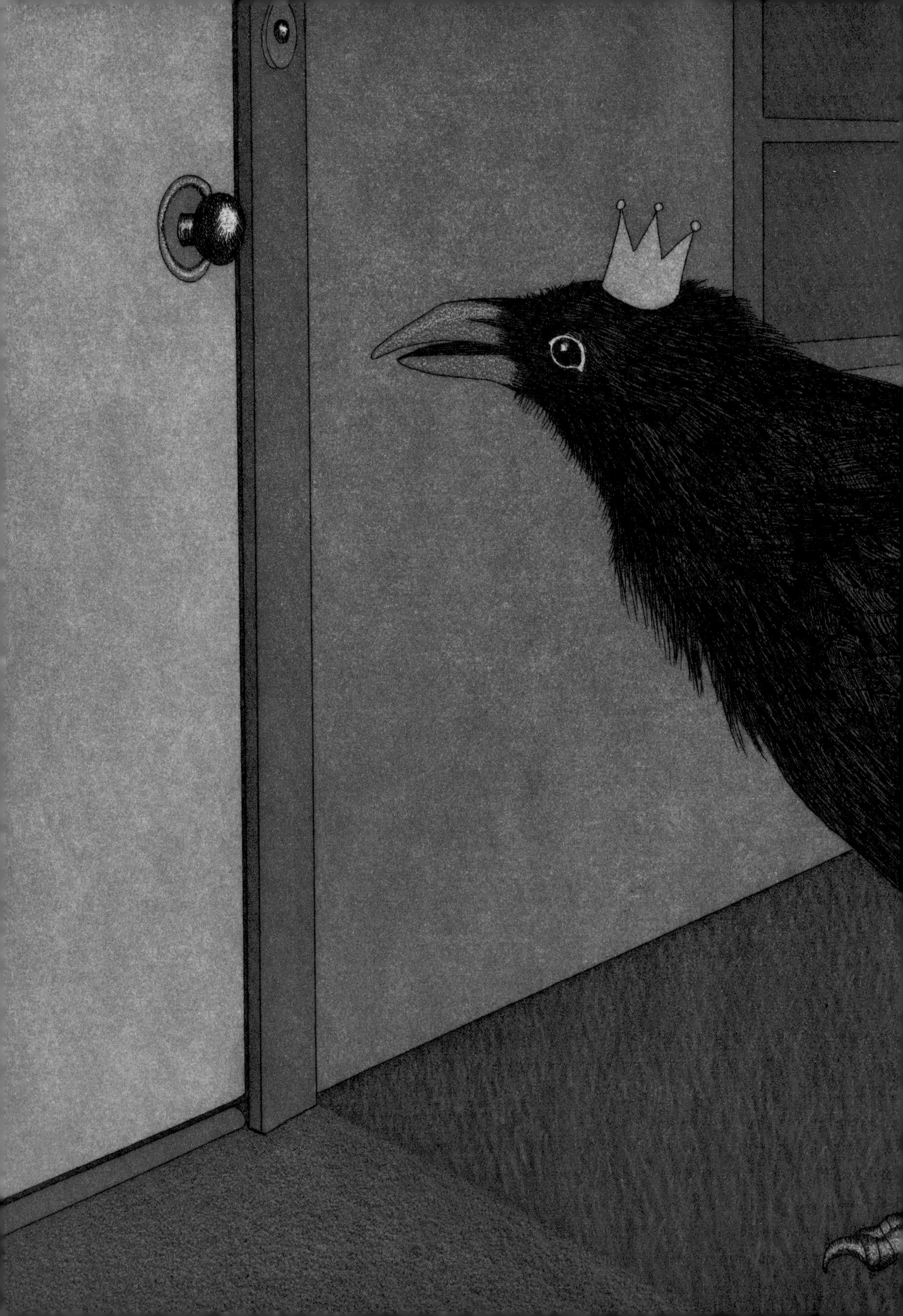

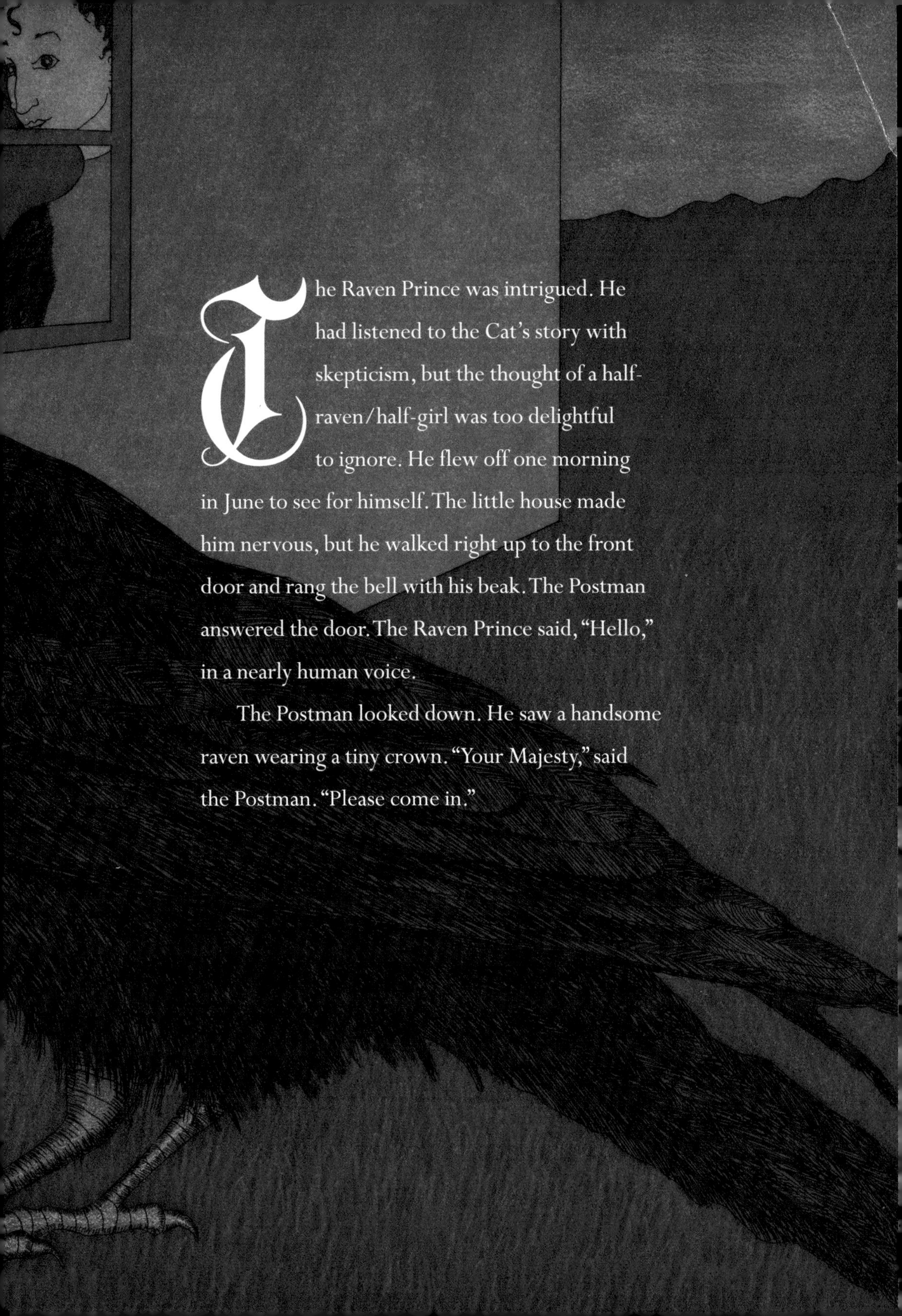

The Raven Prince was intrigued. He had listened to the Cat's story with skepticism, but the thought of a half-raven/half-girl was too delightful to ignore. He flew off one morning in June to see for himself. The little house made him nervous, but he walked right up to the front door and rang the bell with his beak. The Postman answered the door. The Raven Prince said, "Hello," in a nearly human voice.

The Postman looked down. He saw a handsome raven wearing a tiny crown. "Your Majesty," said the Postman. "Please come in."

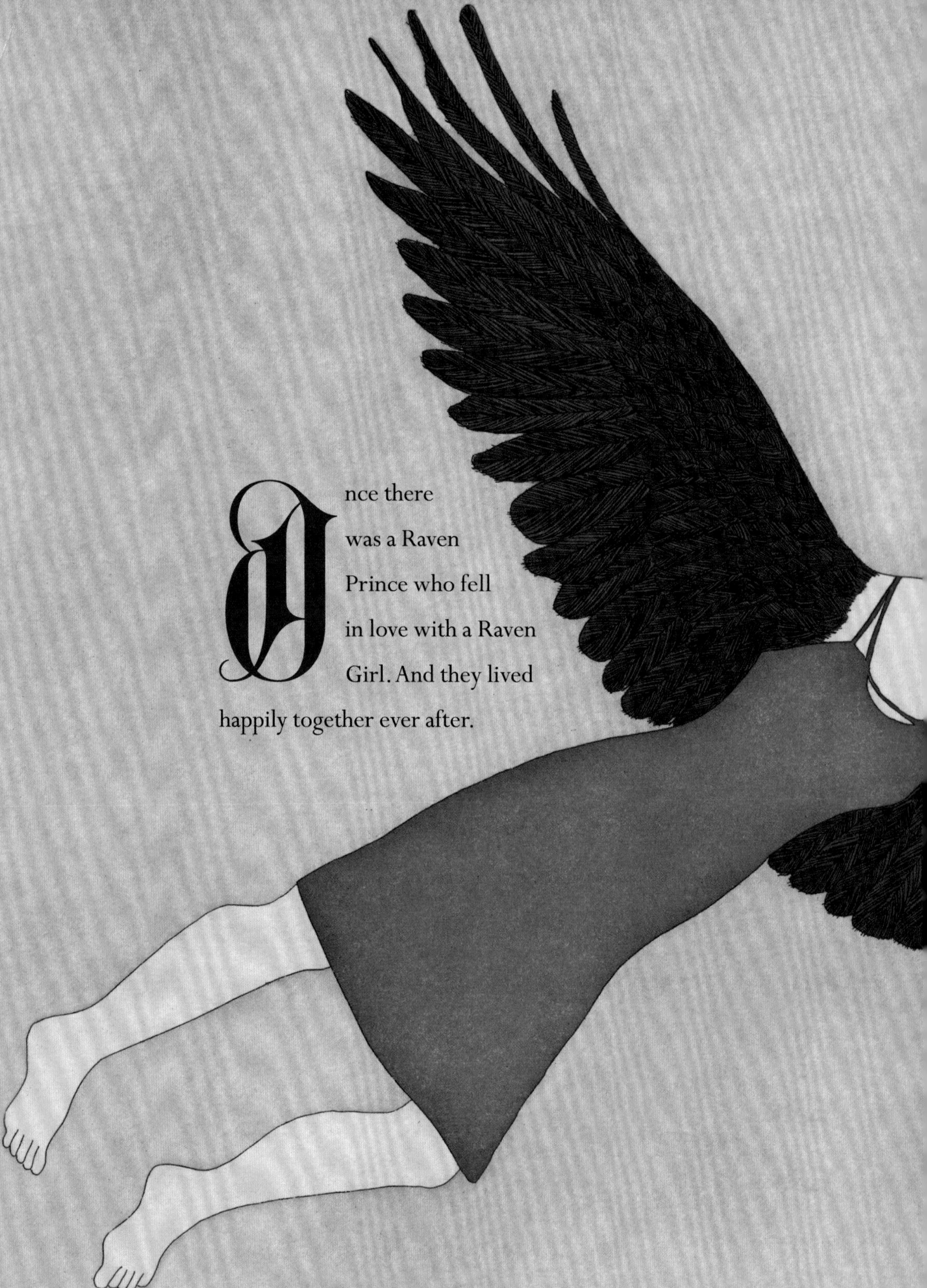

Once there was a Raven Prince who fell in love with a Raven Girl. And they lived happily together ever after.

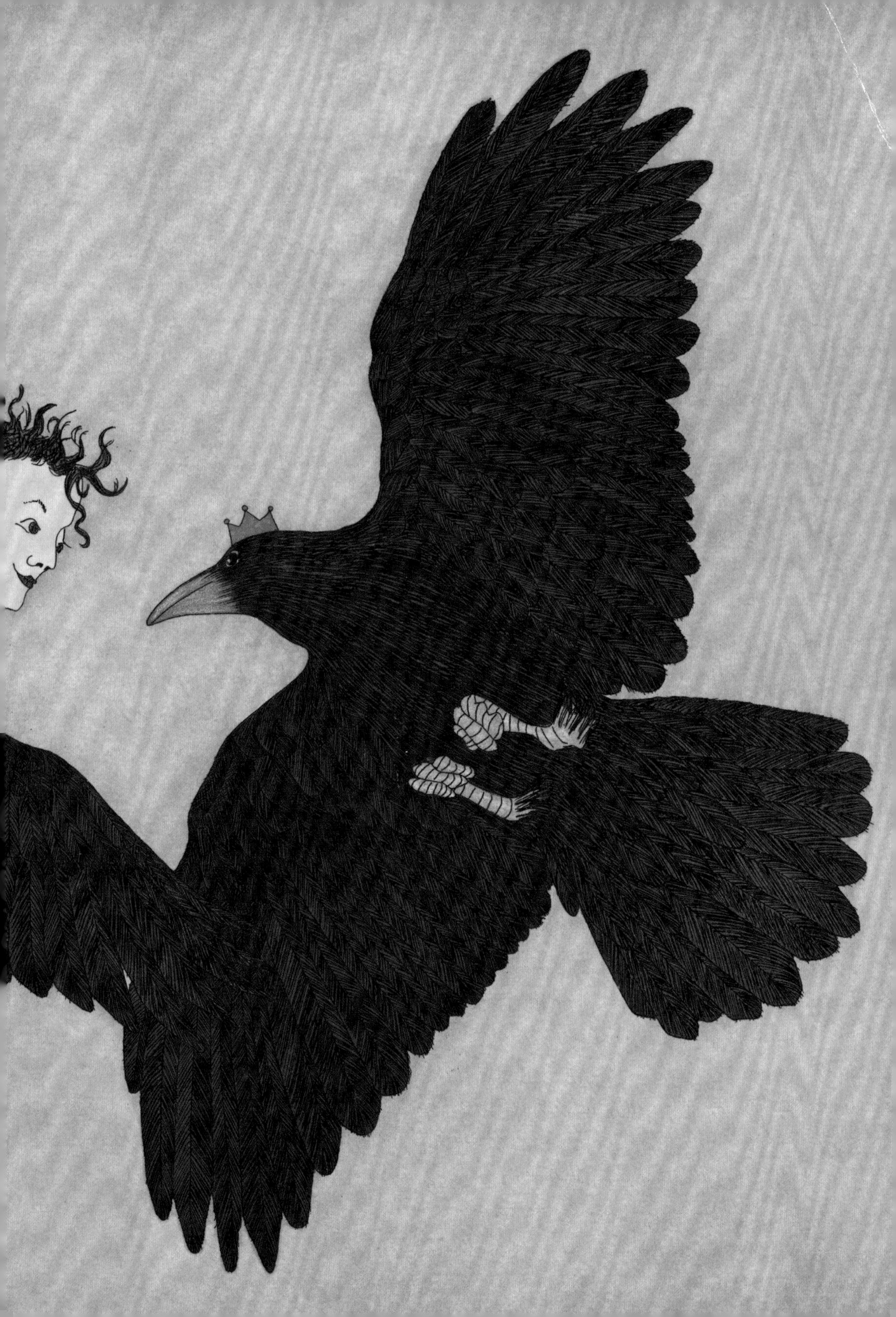

ACKNOWLEDGEMENTS

A while ago, Wayne McGregor invited me to collaborate with him to make a new dance. Wayne is the resident choreographer of the Royal Ballet in London; he would make the dance, I would make the story that would be the beginning point for the dance. I asked Wayne what sort of story he would like and he said, *a new fairy tale.*

Fairy tales have their own remorseless logic and their own rules. *Raven Girl*, like many much older tales, is about the education and transformation of a young girl. It also concerns unlikely lovers, metamorphoses, dark justice, and a prince, as well as the modern magic of technology and medicine. So here is the new fairy tale, ready to undergo its own transformation into dance.

Thank you to Wayne McGregor for the intense and inspiring collaboration. This book is for you.

Thank you to Kevin O'Hare, Monica Mason, David Drew, and the whole team at the Royal Opera House.

Thank you to Tamar Brazis, my editor at Abrams, for letting me run amok and for keeping the whole project running smoothly. Sara Corbett designed this book; thank you for your beautiful (and very quick) work. And thanks to Charlie Kochman, Chad Beckerman, and Michael Jacobs of Abrams for your help and support.

Thank you to Dan Franklin of Jonathan Cape, always, again. And thank you to Markus Hoffmann, Lauren Pearson, and Joseph Regal for making it happen. It is always a pleasure, even when it's pretty crazy.

Thank you to the North Shore Art League for the use of their intaglio studio.

And thanks best and last to Ken Gerleve, my friend and studio assistant, for your printing, patience, organization, hard work, and excellent design advice. It is a delight to work with you.

I hope to see y'all at the dance . . .

AUDREY NIFFENEGGER
SEPTEMBER 27, 2012